Century of Clouds

Century of Clouds

BRUCE BOONE

Preface by ROB HALPERN
New Afterword by BRUCE BOONE

NIGHTBOAT BOOKS   Callicoon, NY

An edition of *Century of Clouds* was published by Hoddypoll Press in 1980.

Cover: *Study of Cumulus Clouds*, 1822 by John Constable. Yale Center for British Art, New Haven, CT / The Bridgeman Art Library
Interior & cover design: typeslowly [cjmattison@gmail.com]

Library of Congress Cataloging-in-Publication Data:

Boone, Bruce.
Century of clouds / Bruce Boone ; preface by Rob Halpern ; new afterword by Bruce Boone.
p. cm.
ISBN 978-0-9822645-2-2 (alk. paper)
I. Title.
PS3552.O6437C46 2009
818.5407--dc22
2009040477

Distributed by University Press of New England
One Court Street
Lebanon, NH 03766
www.upne.com

Nightboat Books
Callicoon, New York
www.nightboat.org

CONTENTS

Preface

Rob Halpern

*"My theme probably has most to do with a very strong feeling
that telling stories actually has an effect on the world."*

It's no exaggeration to call Bruce Boone's *Century of Clouds* one of the
great fugitive works of prose from the late twentieth century. Published
nearly thirty years ago, in 1980, it returns now like a lost contemporary,
speaking as a friend among friends. Despite the passing of time —
to which the title refers, almost as if the work were anticipating its
belated readers — *Century of Clouds* speaks to us here in the present
with its direct address, its stories still navigating the unmapped space
between bodily sensation and critical thought, stimulating so many
intensities — the desire for friendship, the demand for social change
— desires that are ours now, just as they were Boone's then.

Before I discovered *Century of Clouds* in the mid-1990s, this book was
for me a vague rumor, a bit of hearsay associated with an equally vague
literary movement called "New Narrative." I couldn't quite discern the
shape of New Narrative with much clarity then, let alone grasp its
history, but I had already apprenticed myself to it, albeit unwittingly,

by hungrily devouring Robert Glück's classic, *Jack the Modernist*, and trying to imitate its sentences, its tone. Glück's books led me to Boone's collection of short narratives, *My Walk With Bob*, published by Boone's and Glück's own Black Star Series in 1979, and recently reissued by Ithuriel's Spear. Unlike *Century of Clouds*, which was impossible to find, *My Walk With Bob* would occasionally turn up on the "Gay and Lesbian" shelf at Community Thrift on Valencia Street, where I still buy copies whenever I find them for friends. With *Jack the Modernist*, *My Walk With Bob* offered me a set of values — even if I couldn't yet identify them — at once literary and social, combining the emotional intimacy of friendship with the intellectual commitment of critical theory, each stimulating and moderating the other's excesses. And as soon as I was able to identify Glück with the "Bob" of Boone's title, I felt as though I had discovered an important piece of gossip, which drew me deeper into a still unnamable communion.

But nothing prepared me for the revelation of *Century of Clouds* where the seduction of artifice and the rhetoric of critique yield a rare extravagance, which Boone marshals to create new possibilities of social fact. I found the book unexpectedly one day in 1995 while browsing the shelves of the James Hormel Gay and Lesbian Center at the then new San Francisco Public Library. The library's copy was for "reference use only," and while I considered smuggling it out of the building — convinced for a moment that I'd be recovering valuable evidence of a historical event otherwise impossible to prove (a thief in recovery, my acquisitiveness still expressed itself in delusional fantasies of "liberating" meaningful objects) — I decided instead to read it there, and I fell into the book as into a dream, my spine hard against the wall as I slid to the floor where I sat motionless, absorbed. Two hours later I emerged sensing the shape of a world — was it this world? — where writing and desire, friendship and critique, become one another equally and reciprocally to inform a politics. It was one of those life-changing reading experiences when you don't know exactly what's happening to you, but you know that you're never going to be the same. Even now, after having read *Century of Clouds* countless times, a trace of that experience remains, at once profoundly familiar, and still quite strange, a sign that the book has yet to exhaust its promise. Indeed, its affect keeps irrupting in a gray zone of unclassifiable feeling — that pink opaque between body and brain — just on the other side of codified emotion.

❋

Faithful to the imperatives of Gay Liberation, *Century of Clouds* arouses social desires and political demands, which can never be cleanly separated insofar as desire and politics penetrate one another at the root. While reading, I feel such pleasure, as well as an insistence that the world wake from its nightmare, and that it actually *could*, were we only to shake it hard enough. The spirited optimism of Boone's writing tempers the pessimism of its intellect, and that optimism is as infectious as a friend's joy. In *Century of Clouds*, writing, pleasure, gossip, scandal, and emotion *writ large* are full of radical possibilities. Friendship becomes the fundamental unit of political engagement, just as politics reveals its erotics, and storytelling communicates the relationship between them. In every one of Boone's sentences — which move so gracefully between perception and idea, ardor and action — you can feel narrative generating the connective tissue that links community discourse and historical process, readying and toning our attentions, listening for, if not instigating, an unexpected outbreak of history.

Century of Clouds foregrounds emotion, it even *indulges* it, stimulating and formalizing its sensations in such a way that they might be recognized and felt collectively as they are just becoming perceptible. The writing thus engages in a kind of activism, as it organizes so many feelings — intensities of joy and rage, longing and loss, ambivalence and determination, tenderness and aggression — while guiding thought toward a critical assessment of itself, registering the emergence of otherwise unrecorded affects and unanalyzed passions, all of which contain the critical potential to activate social movements. Borrowing a key phrase from Raymond Williams, one can think of the work's commitment to an emergent "structure of feeling," as it participates in the act of organizing affects and tones in the interest of new historical yearnings and urgencies.

At the same time, the narrative situates itself in relation to a vanishing point of social compression — *violence* — that both limits and exceeds the work's perceptual field. But *Century of Clouds*'s vanishing point may also be our present, from where we can read it as a swansong for a history that never was, an elegy for the lost potential of its own historical moment. In the late 1970s, on the eve of a darkening era that didn't yet see what was coming, an era that would soon be identified with the AIDS crisis around which a post-Gay Liberation activism reorganized itself, Boone's narrative aimed to catalyze another history, one where all the utopian energies contained by gay community and commodity culture alike would find a very different form of social expression in a revolutionized world. But in the time between *Century of Clouds* and our present, the epidemic transformed everything about the gay community: its institutions, its discourse, its body, its political vision, and its potential for radical intervention into society at large. The modes of activism, aggression, tenderness, and care that inspire Boone's narrative with the promise of a transformed future would become the very modalities through which a medically compromised gay body struggled for survival, or bare life. It's this historical irony that makes *Century of Clouds* our belated contemporary, for it allows us to hear, as if for the first time, the unfulfilled possibilities of seventies radicalism as it converged with sexuality and writing. And the traces of this more radical potential continue to smolder, even today as gay politics turns toward more normative ends.

Century of Clouds is one of the inaugural works of New Narrative, which emerged at the end of the 1970s in San Francisco with Boone, Glück, and co-conspirator Steve Abbott at the helm. The movement flourished as a loose confederacy of writers during the '80s and '90s when Sam D'Allesandro, Dodie Bellamy, Kevin Killian, Camille Roy, and Mike Amnasan became affiliated with the group by way of Glück's legendary writing workshop, the group's laboratory and marsh. Kathy Acker and Dennis Cooper were New Narrative's fellow-travelers, just as Georges Bataille was its guru. New Narrative continues to inspire the work of a new generation of writers like Jocelyn Saidenberg, David Buuck, Kathy Lou Schultz, and Robin Tremblay-McGaw — all of whom I met in the final years of Glück's workshop — as well as Renee Gladman, Taylor Brady, Magdelena Zurawski, Mary Burger, and others, whose writing explores the convergence of avant-garde poetics and narrativity, critique and storytelling, where the body, together with the social apparatuses that enable and limit it, occupies a critical place.

Writing at the intersection of Gay Liberation, the New Left, and a writing scene that seemed at times unresponsive to the urgencies articulated by sexual politics, writers like Boone and Glück — together with Abbott, who was perhaps responsible for giving New Narrative a name — wanted to animate what Walter Benjamin refers to in his essay "The Storyteller" as the "tiny fragile human body," which Benjamin diagnoses as having been severed from the scene of its own narration, an effect of WWI and the unprecedented traumas of modern life. Benjamin's manner of combining lyricism and critique, autobiography and theory, offered a model, and the ideas proposed in "The Storyteller" are particularly germane to the movement's concerns. New Narrative valorized the body's fragility, restoring its ability to make sense of itself in social space through storytelling, returning to the body a sense of scale by situating it within a dynamic field of social relations — friendship, work, community, commodity, history, futurity — relations that modernity, with its military and industrial prerogatives, had progressively instrumentalized and mystified. *Century of Clouds* is exemplary in this regard, as it makes the questions and concerns that motivated a literary movement legible: how does one relate one's life to social phenomena whose scale threatens to eclipse us? what is the relation between sexual politics and global disasters? who is privileged to speak of these things? with what language? Boone responds to these questions with a voice informed, on the one hand, by the poetry of Frank O'Hara, Jack Spicer, and John Wieners; and, on the other, by the radical gay critiques of Guy Hocquenghem and Mario Mieli. The convergence of these antecedents yields a finely attuned engagement with popular culture, leftist critique, avant-garde writing, and liberatory politics.

✂

From its inception, New Narrative was entangled with an avant-garde poetry scene that was then consolidating itself under the sign of "Language Poetry," and whose activity in the Bay Area during the late 1970s was already a force that any serious writer in conversation with the history of the avant-garde would have had to acknowledge. Against the grain of modernist formalisms, including Language Poetry's strong critique of signification, New Narrative recovered and amplified the otherwise degraded roles of story and emotion as the critical mediums through which the volatile and contested material of real communities circulated. At the same time, New Narrative wanted to retool narrative practice, not so much for its expressive value — not merely to represent a generic "gay story" — but rather for narrative's potential to reflect critically on the performative act of storytelling itself, its role in constructing the storyteller as well as the community to which the storyteller belonged. Pushing beyond the horizon of modernist techniques — a horizon that too often eclipses a locatable body — New Narrative turned to storytelling in an effort to return our living labor to living speech.

Despite divergent priorities — Language Poetry's commitment to form and the social implications of textuality, signification, method; New Narrative's commitment to story, and the politics of sex, scandal, community — New Narrative nevertheless shared aspects of Language writing's critique of ideology (the seeming transparency of the word, the so-called self-evidence of the voice), while pushing beyond that critique. Drawing attention to this convergence and divergence of concerns in his editor's note prefacing the second issue of *Soup* magazine in 1980, Steve Abbott introduced the new approach to storytelling like this: "New Narrative is language conscious, but arising out of specific social and political concerns of specific communities." In other words, the writing is attentive to linguistic surface while also grounding itself in community-based political interests. Abbott goes on to emphasize New Narrative's challenge to the prevalent idea that writing associated with struggling communities ought not be experimental for fear of risking accessibility, that is, the notion that innovative writing practices and movement politics were somehow mutually exclusive. He notes how New Narrative "stresses the enabling role of content in determining form rather than stressing form as independent, separate from its social origins and needs," making a very different argument that new social demands can only find adequate expression by way of new forms. And *Century of Clouds* takes this argument a step further still: it is precisely by way of emergent forms that such demands become audible for the first time.

⌘

"These thoughts large and public, how to relate them to my life? How to link with experience that touches — only rarely — my past? To tell about desiring, too. Perhaps a beginning to tell you stories." Boone's New Narrative form answers that "how?" and it moves a little like this: In order to tell you the story of X, I'll need first to tell you the story of Y, within which, as you'll see, I find myself talking about Z in a manner I can no longer stand by. The reason for my change of stance is illuminated by the story itself, so I ought to begin by telling you all about that. Be forewarned, however, that in the course of relating these events, I'll need to step outside the various artifices I've devised — the story's appearance of coherent progression, all those transitions meant to make my artful coherence believable — in order to reflect on the relation between formal ideas and thematic content. And so: "I'd like to tell you a little about ideology now — or rather, my ideas on the subject — by telling you about my past, about the time of my first realizations on this peculiar function of language."

With such a formal strategy, the writing is able to mobilize an array of themes in a manner motivated at once by urgency and caprice, and Boone's themes range from gay sexuality to leftist organizing, feminism to friendship, spirituality to grief. Its self-reflexive form of storytelling elaborates a running commentary on itself, a method Boone has referred to as "text-metatext," and this allows the work to sustain a critical meditation on its own intervention as both an aesthetic and a political practice. Storytelling thus becomes performative — "You want what you write to actually cause these things to come to exist, you don't want just to describe them," Boone writes — an aesthetic act capable of mapping and transforming its own conditions of possibility. The writing doesn't only aim to express the voice of an already existing community, but also to call a potential community into being, one in which we, as readers, are invited to participate.

❡

Much of *Century of Clouds'* material revolves around events and interventions set at the annual conclave of the Marxist Literary Group, which convened in St. Cloud, Minnesota over the course of two summers, 1977 and 1978. Boone names names, and while we may not know who Alex, Robbie and Christine are, the reputations of Fred, Terry, and Stanley exceed the frame of the story (Jameson, Eagleton, and Aronowitz, respectively). Naming names is just one way in which New Narrative elevates gossip to a literary strategy that sees itself consequentially engaged with really existing social ecologies. "I wanted people to feel they had a stake in this writing and credit it and affirm it and give it a community and social life it could only have if many people saw their representations there, not just one person," Boone writes, and continues, "Your text could not begin until others were able to start loving and hating you on account of it. Finally, I wanted a text so tangled up with others that it would be their intentions, and not mine, that gave it such place as it would have in a large social history."

Gossip is one way in which a community registers its own history. It is neither a substitute for emotion nor a prosthetic for critique, but a social practice through which both emotion and critique are lived. Like the community's unconscious yielding to its own vernacular analysis, gossip helps us to hear what can and can't be said in the interest of transgressing those limits. Gossip challenges its own generic constraints, and so does New Narrative as it practices the story as a form of "essay," which simply means an attempt, in the sense of a wager, or a risk. This approach to storytelling is crucial to New Narrative's ethos for restoring us to relation — to one another (friendship: you and me), to the group (community: us), to global disasters under late capitalism (history), and to the shared hope for another future.

Whatever that other future might be, it requires an intervention in the present. *Century of Clouds* both narrates and performs such an intervention — like a utopian breach in time — depicting a series of consequential interruptions at the level of the story's content (intervention as theme), while performing an interruption in expectations about what narrative can do (intervention as form). But in Boone's approach to storytelling, and in New Narrative generally, intervention aims to do something more, something verging on the impossible: to narrate the interruptions in its own narration, to tell the story of its lacunae, its hesitations and its holes, and to push narrative toward what can't be narrated, due to social constraints, and physiological limits. Or, as Glück puts it in his "Long Note on New Narrative," "to arrive at ecstasy and loss of narration as the self sheds its social identities."

With respect to the social concerns that inspire *Century of Clouds*, intervention means direct action on the material organization of social space and the dynamics that sustain it. In this sense, the narrative's form and the story's content realize what Guy Hocquenghem calls "the special characteristic of the homosexual intervention to make what is private — sexuality's little secret — intervene in public, in social organization," instigating the breakdown of the terms upon which the stability of that organization depends. Just as Boone's narrative proposes intervention as the practical means for affecting change in real community politics — from minor gestures like pinning a little pink triangle to one's tee shirt, which unexpectedly causes "a situation no one expected" at the Marxist Literary Group's summer conclave, to disrupting group processes in order to make social needs audible that are otherwise silenced — the book becomes the intervention about which it speaks, as it raises its own interruptions to new levels of understanding.

Century of Clouds is nothing short of a full-blown realization of these New Narrative strategies. Even thirty years after its first publication, it offers us a critical model, at once topical and useful not only for its literary historical value, but because it remains our untimely contemporary. In Boone's storytelling, we can feel our own historical potential, sometimes with uncanny familiarity, as if a whole register of emotional life that was emergent in the late 1970s has since become vestigial within our own structure of feeling, haunting us like a spectral presence. Or, as if the foreclosed possibilities of all that was incipient thirty years ago contain affects whose residues still cling to our own social aspirations, stimulating disoriented desires that feel new to us. With its return now to a new readership — across a dark divide, where it offers us a vehicle for transport — Boone's New Narrative resumes its place as our guide and companion.

Century of Clouds

I like the bigness of things, their largeness. Dreaming my favorite dream I'm flying above an enchanted forest, arms stretched out wide. The trees are emerald green and the fields under me ordered in neat yellow squares. They shout and compete with each other for the splendor of it. High above me there's a clear sapphire sky. Oh the serenity! Now I shift the bones of my wrist and slightly turn. Facing the sun I begin my descent.

In the years of friendship I see those I love in mosaic-like patterns, and me along with them. Who will ever know our names in a hundred years! We're like the catalogs of flora, and moving toward a brilliant future. Wave upon wave of collective life displaying ever new patterns. Like the stripes of sea bass; like the desert cactus in bloom after years of waiting. It's spring, and the acacias are beginning to carpet the streets with their yellow polleny fuzz. Patterns, designs, excesses I love. At night I look up to emptiness, and the Milky Way is a ribbon of distant faces turned outward, still asleep. Will they wake?

At the institute last summer I dreamt for several nights about Fred's repeated anecdote. By sheer coincidence, he says, when three had come together, Sartre is the first to speak. 'Three little men!' — and a smile to Picasso and Charlie Chaplin. I dream they're in a circle looking down, peering into and beyond something. But it's there at their feet. I wake up and laugh. I have to tell Fred this! He's so large, like the world. Everyone will enjoy my dream joke.

There's an explosion when I think these thoughts. Letelier is being blown up in his car by the agents of Chilean reaction. The sound of nearly silent bullets — and 9 black men are dead in Oakland from police assassination. Racism; poverty. Lives of women and gays oppressed in patriarchy. Daily violence done to workers. A workers' movement now bloody and sundered with wounds.

These thoughts large and public, how to relate them to my life? How to link with experience and touches — only rarely — my past? To tell about desiring too.

Perhaps beginning to tell you stories. Some important friendships, in between spaces as my life moves outward. Problems. Questions.

First let me tell you about David. David, who was in many ways the one person I should have gotten to know earlier and better before the summer institute was over. He was also as it turned out — surprising for a straight man — the best of us all at gossip. Oh gossip of his own kind to be sure! And I should add it was hardly ours — that is, Alex's and mine and Robbie's. David's anecdote of the funeral of a party militant at Père Lachaise is an example. Another drab anecdote of Party life, you would think. But imagine the effect. Taking everyone by surprise, as David would point out, the boss himself came. The chef de parti and patron. Thorez.

Now those were the days! — David would groan, leaving it to the listener to decide whether he was ironic or sad — though I always thought both. Thorez had arrived to speak personally, it seems, in tribute to the lifelong militant service of the deceased. As a footnote to the story David explained that the Party had then started buying up sections of the cemetery's wall as a burial place for distinguished rank and file of party bureaucrats. The wall had an illustrious past. It was the place the last Communards had been taken to be shot.

But here I'll interrupt, to try to give you a better sense of the direction of this talk. That afternoon David and I had walked along the Mississippi together discussing the many difficulties that come up in building counter-hegemony institutions for the great moments in existence — the problematic but necessary ceremonies, you might say, involved in constructing a proletarian culture. No small subject, we both agreed, for a leisurely afternoon stroll. What might such a thing mean, aside from its obvious distortion — the culture of a party? I asked David for examples, since he was the one with the experience in that department. He drew on the practice of the Italian and French parties. I was then regaled with anecdote after anecdote, all of which displayed a lively interest in the rhetorical arts as well as a true and serious concern for their subject.

But now the conversation took an eccentric turn. What . . . we asked ourselves with the morbid zest of schoolmen or Talmudic scholars, do you do exactly when you can't really have a Christian funeral any more or a bourgeois one? The question referred back to our subject in this way. We meant — how can you have ceremonies at all anymore, though indeed how can you not? Who could imagine a 'Marxist' funeral? — we wondered. And don't the trappings of power and terror remain exactly that, occasions of expediency and vehicles for domination? — though still, when you get down to basics, the necessary arrangements of our day, indispensable to the transitional times of history. *Omnis caro ad te veniat!* As the saints used to exclaim, in the disconcertingly naïve hope that nothing is ever lost finally. We didn't go so far as to say, A toast to death! but we were nostalgic for the victories of abstract thought and the ways that ceremony pays tribute to that thought. These were my own real feelings. That I can assure you. And perhaps they were David's too.

That was how I first began to think about the problem of bureaucracies, and as usual my approach was indirect. My conversations with David were enhanced by an awareness of his particular situation, being affiliated with a party. This meant I could be sure of a continuing and lively interest in these talks on David's part. Our personal histories guaranteed that each talk would have its successor. And they did. Yet for me the problem was, and is, a more intimate one — it involves accounting for a large sense of loss in life. I can't burden myself with its duty to sadness without first conjuring it and recounting it in anecdote after anecdote, accumulating kindnesses to match its own and wrapping it in language with the layers that decency demands. Wrapped so tight, won't that loss rebuke its bonds and leap out to new life, transformed? In my view anyone's piety in writing their stories rests on this. Without need, who would write? Or do politics? Or believe in the power of names?

But let me return you to the story I was telling you. David and I usually crossed back to the campus by way of an iron suspension bridge that spans the river right after Mille Lac. The river is still relatively narrow and the bridge is picturesque. We would often pause for a rest and smell the mysterious water smells as the river eddied and stirred around the willows and dank river plants along its shores. David's manner would become refreshed, invigorated again. Still characteristically restrained David would gesture as he talked. His hand and arm movements alluded to Thorez's French oratorical style. On these body movements I felt I could read a combination of David's respect for the late party boss's real accomplishments as well as a parody or critique of the Stalinism which was the historical reason for their existence. And in these gestures too I felt the ambiguous quality that gave David's best stories their intelligent wit. At this point David was portraying the *patron* as a comic Mayor Daley — a kingpin, the man who once could have stopped all the factories in France overnight, kept the train from running if he wanted to, brought everything to a halt. David's picture of the CP chief ended, in my recollection, with the following scene — Thorez raising his finger to heaven and invoking *la patrie*. Fatherland? But how can one listen to such things in a party leader? Yet here's the peculiar thing, David says, there were tears in everyone's eyes. They were really moved by him. Then we lost ourselves in our respective meditations, David apparently in some further reverie his own story had brought on, while I, in a completely uninterested fashion, had begun to think about my graduate school years. Meanwhile David and I had almost reached the dorms and the pleasant warmth of the afternoon had begun to dull our critical faculties. I felt content and had blocked out my previous objections to the blandness and repetitive qualities of this Midwest landscape. I made up my mind to accept these very un-California-like yellows and greens and clear slate blues as the provisional evidence of a genuine American-ness. We had reached the scraggly lawns, elm tree groupings and well spaced brick buildings of the campus itself. In a mood of great peacefulness we sauntered along the curving path to the dorms, feeling the lovely Midwest summer lapping around us. But our mood was not destined to last. Just as we rounded the corner of our dorm building a volleyball flew by our noses. An irritatingly exuberant, cheerful middle-aged college teacher followed. With great puffs and pants he told us that our comrades had begun their afternoon volleyball game, and that we were invited to join them. The afternoon's mood was shattered, and it appeared that it was our fate to become part of the game.

But may I ask your permission to break off for the time being? I'd like to postpone that particular volleyball game to a later time when I can give you a developed account of my part in it as well as a larger explanation of the tensions it attempted to cover over but ended up exacerbating. Be patient. I promise you the events in their fullest significance. You'll hear more of this famous game!

As for the Thorez of David's story, I want to make one admission. If the ancient CP boss didn't actually use the word *patrie* as transpires in my version of the story, he might as well have. The story is a critique. It is meant to contribute to a discussion of future choices. That is my conscious meaning in retelling it.

I am aiming at something more important that Maurice Thorez's character deficiencies or, more seriously, the historical Cominform policies he is usually thought to embody in those critical post-War years — when, as a child, I was blissfully ignorant of these graver issues. Eisenhower was president, and I moved among the appliances and commodities of that era with the sense of abstraction that life and my parents encouraged in me. It was a sense of things I willingly capitulated to, and it gave my temperament its determining cast, as it did for so many others during the time. Remembering these stories of David and of the institute, I merge with that dazed child of the

Eisenhower years. I become all bright and murky and fuzzy and pain-
less, a distant thought about myself I get on off days in a pleasant act
of mourning that doesn't know itself. The Pole Star of a temperament,
this thought may or may not lead, as events themselves will prove, to
some genuine future — vindicating all the dead and in the process
freeing the past of it garrulity. Like the work of mourning described
in textbooks, mine too is a real work. In temporary ill health it refuses
praxis to see the problem clearly. In such a stalemate isn't one tempted
to see beauty? What comes next then? Thinking — and more thinking. A collaboration with an enemy. Well, yes; but sometimes activism
is too, so the problem isn't always simple. You see, when commodity
society burst into my soul like I Love Lucy on TV, I wasn't at all prepared. Thought came to me dressed up in a kitsch polka-dot dress
with make-up on and a carrot red wig like Lucy Ricardo. Oh beautiful
life of the mind!

Now here's my view of David at the conference table. Strange
how he introduces his Gramsci talk . He begins epigraphically, he cites
a political cartoon from one of the Italian bourgeois papers. You see
that it's someplace in Rome, it's PCI headquarters. Stacked high are
official portraits of Gramsci, gathering dust in the clutter of papers
and filing cabinets. Above a desk is another picture; it's Stalin. This is
what the cartoon caption says — 'We were only kidding!' Ah-ha-ha,
oh ha-ha-ha. You should have seen us then, it really got us. We practically died laughing! But afterwards I wondered if the joke was gallows
humor or in the spirit of Gramsci's own slogan — 'Pessimism of the
intellect, optimism of the will.' David's Gramsci talk at least succeeded in brightening up the issue of bureaucracy. But it didn't answer all
my questions. It didn't solve a number of problems.

A person might wonder how relevant Gramsci is these days. Would he for instance have foreseen the state of the PCI today? To me the polarization of the institute was Stalin vs. Gramsci, and the atmosphere at our conference table was often an uneasy one. Humorous, yes. Though with a constant edge. Our humor acknowledged a continual dissatisfaction but reassured by asking us, 'we can still talk about all this, can't we?' Implicit was the convergence of our personal histories. And what about Robbie's long, meandering joke about the elderly Jewish tailor who brings in the message from Trotsky? — 'Stalin, you were right. I was wrong!' the punch line amusing us because it presupposed people's whole lives in militancy. In such jokes a community is heard declaiming its language practice and relaxing. This community goes on to dream like any other of its successes and failures — and makes plans for a future.

It is a future to which I want to refer with this writing. I believe and hope that among the present crises we prepare for it. But when the time comes, won't we find ourselves on the hither side of that boundary? — with others going on ahead, new pioneers themselves. How will we be present to that absence? Declining to instrumentalize those gone before us, can we hope that those still to come will go further — and raise us up alive?

The orthodox Catholic LeRoy Ladurie describes a minor character in the medieval village of Montaillou in this way. 'Arnaud Genis was reasonably well off and probably owned his own house. He was not a glutton for work, and liked to sit in the sun. He was employed as a canon's servant and subsequently as an assistant sacristan. But his chief role, like that of the modern historian, was to act as a mouthpiece for the dead.' Turned on its head, I wonder, might this function describe a more honorable and future calling? — one we might think of as a guarding of the necropolis of this world. The monition takes on an urgently practical form in a well known essay by the social critic Walter Benjamin. 'Even the dead,' Benjamin warns, 'will not be safe from the enemy if he wins — and this enemy has not ceased to be victorious.' What such philosophers as these say may or may not be true, but the truth value of their remarks in my view remains in an ability to perform for us an important service. They yield a slipperiness that escapes the bailiff pursuing them. That bailiff is death.

Somewhere at the limit of this line of thinking was what I thought of as David's wit. I would call it 'Communist camp' and 'hard-core' — though this last phrase belongs to Fred, who, as I recall was partial to it ambiguously, insofar as it might also be known as 'writerly.' But that is another story; and if I get to it at all it will be later. I liked David's sense of humor because it seemed to heighten and illuminate the social dimension of things. His jokes were about people with determined life spans, and if it doesn't seem too grim to say it, they were like small memento moris designed to urge the listener to make a good, more human use of his time. The best of this 'Communist camp' came from the period David had spent travelling abroad. It must have been an isolated year for him, and not just from the point of view of 'party discipline.' The result, however, was a further contribution to the art of storytelling in David's own French moralist style. How do you explain the absurd customs of foreigners? You make them more absurd until they get to be interesting. You fabricate. Later, mandarin critics will attempt to show their students how such apparently amusing stories are really polemics against the social evils of the times. Naturally the students will reject these explanations. They will have contempt for such writings and hate them. When the revolution comes the students will know what course to take. They will denounce all literature as amusement and entertainment; and in this they will be more correct than they know. Brecht lays special emphasis on the theme in his Little Organon for the Theater when he points out that revolutionary literature must be pleasing. Fault-finders of course rebuke such a doctrine as meretricious, insalubrious. It implies, they say, that literature might be likened to travelling circuses, street entertainments or other low diversions. But David's high French style, I own, laid emphasis on precisely these ornamental values. That makes sense to me but then wit is said to come only too naturally to intellectuals and apparatchiks — the ones who live by ordering signs. What do you think?

During his year abroad David had come up with an interesting but eccentric theory which purported to be a way of accounting for what he had seen. It had in it a lot of David, I thought. An explanation of ideological practices that remained an arbitrary one, it nonetheless turned out to be surprisingly workable. David's theory was a fantasy and meant to entertain; and hearing it I envisaged an alternate youth — other and non-existent student years in David's life. First the long, boring years of home and family. Dark, depressing London! Then at last the big chance! The excitement of meeting brilliant new friends at one of the universities, etc. You are introduced to J.M. Keynes. What a strange new life this is! Theories abound. What if, for instance — just an idea, mind you — one might maintain high employment rates *and* control inflation at the same time . . . by increasing public expenditures! Preposterous! Yet slowly, the idea gains credence. It may be a harebrained idea, my dear, but as I told Virginia only yesterday — it works. Indeed! chimes in Leonard with absent-minded admiration.

Just so. For a short moment, this was the David I saw sitting at the edge of Peter's bed, an ironic drawl on his face, ready to open up this hobby-horse of a theory and reveal the inner clockwork mechanism that made it run.

Nor was it the case that David's theory was 'new.' It was just worked out. A person could exactly categorize or type the official pictures of higher party echelons with regard to a limited number of functions. These functions, it turned out, were first schematized by the Orthodox Church. Examples might be color relations, body and head positioning, light symbolism, aura size or shape, the basic 'cut' or drape of the clothing and so on. In official pictures these functions were distributed exactly as they were in the images of saints in the churches. In given icon X for instance, or bureaucratic picture Y, there would be only 12 possible body positions, 5 possible color schemes, etc. A set of rules, or syntax, would govern their combination. You would, in short, find yourself in possession of a genuine French combining mechanism — or *combinatoire*. The theory got really interesting when you got to the national cultures. A Chinese iconography, say, or an Albanian one, might indifferently be submitted to analysis and reveal an identical pattern. With this theory-machine you might look behind Albania and see China, in China discern features of a young U.S.S.R., find the ancient saints Boris and Gleb behind commissars, etc. There would be no originality and no causality, the historical series not being a genetic one. But the real wonder of this theory is that it becomes more and more ahistorical. With delight one sees Marie de Médicis being crowned queen of heaven, her court an extravagant mélange of doctors of the church, winged archangels and seraphim, and gods and goddesses from antiquity. Tableaus of power from the standpoint of utility! Retz in his glory, plotting mutual seditions of parliament, king and parliament could not have done better. And as for the accusation that Marxism has no theory of politics, let the Poulantzases of our times look back as serenely to a Gallic past as Gramsci once did to an Italian one! With a theory like this, all ages are our contemporaries.

From orthodoxy's viewpoint, however, one might ask if David's theory had strayed from the normative, blameless pastures of irony to the rough-and-tumble ground of sarcasm, in which offense is boldly given and ruffians lie in wait for the unwary. Did this theory challenge the powers-that-be? To counter charges of red-baiting I admit to systematizing what were in fact a few random observations, taking them out of context, working them up to a consistent viewpoint. In this way I want to present the disadvantages as well as advantages of such critiques of power — for that is really what David's theory was. To put it in other words, we might ask if the call to Communism can be understood by bureaucrats. At what point does the demand for liquidation of state power become incompatible with the tactical and temporary expedient of seizing this same power? Has it been so up to now? Does it remain so? And for how long then? — etc. Those are the questions that such theory brings to mind. Yet speaking on behalf of orthodoxy one might wonder what could distinguish such vocal criticism from ultraleftists or worse, anarchists? And doesn't this critique imply a demise of the vanguard party as we know it? — Lenin's party! We are on dangerous ground here, comrades, dangerous indeed!

In defense of David's theoretic diversions, though, I want to intervene here in my own name and claim that there isn't really a choice at all. The issue has been raised, as they say, by events themselves; the question is not if, but *how* to question power. And it's such a large problem! — because it involves so many aspects of everyday life that we have scarcely begun to think about in this way. Take writing, for instance — an example by the way I love to use! By writing this story I want to make you think about certain political matters — a praiseworthy objective, no? But I also want to amuse and entertain you, and more. In what I write I would like you to be able to feel pleasure, even joy. I don't want to give up on either goal, though only one of them is concerned with power. Isn't it possible to think about power in new ways? Why not suppose that as comradeship and equality get to know each other, they naturally become friends — lovers even. And if — as you must — you consider such problems in your own life, you must soon begin to seriously ask yourself, how is it possible to make a truly human social life for the first time?

Awkwardly, our writerly alternatives are necessarily utopian; they can only be charted negatively as the kinds of language we use. Though it certainly could be worse, our situation — to be sure! — isn't the best of all possible worlds. And no amount of tinkering can change one basic fact — to write is not the same as to act, nor will be in our foreseeable futures. Writings can even be obstacles to future developments; one can so easily think of the regressive, as well as imaginative, side of language in its past behaviors. Yet if a person were to ask me, I would always claim there are reasons enough to hope, if we only see what is actually happening around us. Why not look at the kinds of language that articulate goals of community? — examples of imagination that narrate us toward the new. What Gramscian direction is here! Figuration may be pre-figuration. Yet — too often! — our language continues to be metaphorical with muttered apologies. Why? The tritest similitudes may mark an aspiring dimension toward a future, and metaphors can be quite assertive this way. But they testify to power ambiguously. They are the inefficient instruments of any existing social relations. Thus Sir Philip Sidney reveals himself a Puritan ideologue in bad faith when he defends the instrumental values of the literature of another epoch. 'What is Ulysses in the storm and other sad plights,' he asks with a flourish, 'but exercises in patience and magnanimity that he might shine the brighter in the near following prosperity . . . ?' He correctly desires Christ's objectifying government among the nations, but also fears to relinquish wholly the known subjective pleasures of a literary system he loves. Loving metaphors of Greek literature, he sets up his case for its propaganda value, for Puritanism — and thus serves two masters. If he were Ulysses for our pleasure, he would today be in prison. And on this philosophic terrain others go further. Metaphor, far from being a form of knowledge, is rather the 'occasion of error, the danger to which one exposes oneself when one does not examine the obscure region of confusions' — so says Foucault explaining the rationalist. And dispensing with frippery and ornament, such writers find themselves becoming conscious instruments of Power . . .

But I will admit it — David's theory hardly went this far. It was proposed as a reaction, and even as critique it remained moderate in its claims, confectionary in its outlook, no threat to anyone. What worried me was this — what was its relation to life? 'The hand mill gives you the feudal lord and the steam mill the industrial capitalist' — that's a theory of history I still believe in, to put it bluntly for you. But it's not clear to me even now whether David's theory was more like the steam mill or the capitalist. And if it *wasn't* ideology, then why did I find it so frothy and heady, so fascinating? I hope the socialist life to come will include Sachertorte and Kaffee mit Schlag, my idea of heaven on earth.

I wouldn't like to draw conclusions from just one case, even if I had them. Generally, David's everyday humor was milder and less tendentious, I think, and not as politically specific as the icon theory. And if it was political, it was more like camp, though more gentle, bland even, like the TV humor of the '50s. There was something there of the spurious but courageous wit of Kilgallen, for instance, as she girded herself for battle while the suave m.c. would announce, 'Will you come in and *sign in, please*, mystery guest!' What's My Line, a once-a-week exercise in silk top hat manners, sparkling wit and good-natured bonhomie on a quiz show budget. Later, David was to put his TV fan's knowledge to further good — and camp — use when he began to prepare for our grand finale, the institute's political evening with talks by each of the 6 or 7 parties present. This was dubbed our What's-My-Line evening by David. He thought that an issue as inherently serious as the question of parties and party organization was just not going to be adequately dealt with to anybody's satisfaction, no matter how hard you tried. As I recall, though, the representatives of the sectarian parties didn't share this view. They decided to set aside an evening toward the end of our institute for a forum on the question of membership. Each organization had about 15 minutes to present its line. When all the parties had spoken, you would know which one to join. That was the idea anyway.

And as I think about it, the naivete of the idea embarrasses me. I feel a little embarrassed, I guess, on behalf of the institute; it seems like such an abrupt transition to praxis. But this embarrassment is factitious, since I have more ego strength than that, I don't identify myself with the institute that closely. I feel a more serious embarrassment than that, and the really chagrining aspect of this anecdote lies in a small detail I haven't yet mentioned. I was, myself, one of the most enthusiastic and encouraging about the idea when it first came up. I thought it sounded quite militant, and I thought that in supporting it I would be militant myself.

David was against the idea from the start. What would be accomplished in this night of vaudeville? Indeed. It seemed to me later, it was as if the different parties and organizations were commodities, items on a grocer's shelf, articles of consumption. Each had its own brightly colored label with a competing trade name, each was calling out urgently to the passing customer, 'Choose *me*, choose *me!*', inveigling and tempting you with its own uniquely rich and suggestive 'promesse du bonheur.' For a few cents you might sample the delights of any brand that struck your fancy. The ideologically jaded might even choose one after another without finally sating themselves, true Commodore Perrys of the soul, Magellans rounding the Horn — to use the metaphor freely — of world upon world of disputatious complexity! Party Night, in other words, was a profoundly stupid idea, and to be cynical about it you might have called it a trap of fools.

Myself among them? I've exaggerated the effects but not the principle of the thing. In my opinion Party Night managed to caricature itself that way. I want to ascribe to David a healthy dose of reality awareness, exemplified in his judgment about our evening of organization speeches. And as for me, well, just imagine for yourself someone living and existing and having difficulties with so many ways of thinking that are boring and meaningless or irritating and dumb and just not gratifying. Well. Don't you naturally want to do something about the situation? You want to change it. So you try and try. But there's a brick wall there that notifies you that it doesn't intend to stop being exactly that. And then you realize that it's no good, you might as well not even try at all. And the hollow laughter comes. All those desperate jokes and glittering witty sayings against a black sky which is — one realizes with growing horror — empty! Let me ask you quite frankly — do you know *why* it is empty? Is it empty because of European existentialism for instance? Or — perhaps — because of a broken heart! This is Kermit the Frog speaking now. And he'll be forever pining without realizing it for his glamorous friend, Miss P. Miss P.'s the lucky one though. She's so practical you know she has accessories by Max Factor and no heart at all. What a pointless and confusing love story, dear reader. In order to save it from sexism, we'll change the gender. I'll decide to be Ms. P. myself. You see how it is! Before things get 'cancelled and raised' into socialism, we can only manage to understand the good things to come in some distorted fashion, as a dream. And me? Well, as a gay man, I see myself, plain as ever, in a community of frogs, an amphibious *Gemeinschaft*. Is one of the frogs really me? But I have a scarlet P. on my back! What can it mean! Alarmed and intent on my duty, as always, I begin to trudge up the snowy mountain . . .

Stop that nonsense, you've lost the point completely! You have a story to tell! All right, that's much better. You were saying . . .

That I should probably go back to my Maurice Thorez story. Or maybe I should tell you another Paris story it reminds me of. But first — one further detail about David. Although David is a straight man, I can remember that Alex and Robbie and I did once discuss whether someone ought to try to bring him 'out.' We discussed this idea but eventually rejected it. It was suggested that straight men can surprisingly often have strengths found in gay men. That would be admirable, and honorable! We concluded that in the balance David would do more good for the world by staying straight.

We gay men tend to have a tolerance for ambiguity this way that's often sadly lacking in many straight men in my opinion. And though we don't 'copy' it, we often seem to share this tolerance with women. And here is what I want to ask — isn't the question of women critical for our politics? I believe so myself. And here's an important way this applies even 'outside of' women — hasn't feminism raised the question of people's subjectivity for the first time politically? Last night I went to a political lecture. In deep gloom I learned of suffrage for women in the Weimar years of Germany — I learned how women in great numbers voted for fascism near the end of this time. About gay men the record was still worse — I blushed to hear of records of complicity of many gay organizations. What needs might women have had that were never recognized by left groups then? Weren't gay men attracted by the fascist idea of male camaraderie? What about the economism of the KP, of the SPD of that time? These are vexed questions. But I raise them to testify to my aspirations to have actual effects in real life with these stories. I want to make people think — and then to change the world.

But now for my promise of a Paris story, a story that the anecdote about Thorez reminds me of. David's anecdote about the CP chief would have taken place in the '50s, about the time — it now occurs to me irrelevantly — that I was in Europe myself. This was when I was visiting Jeanne Baudrillard and had a letter of introduction from my mother. As a young woman my mother was supposed to be under Jeanne's 'sponsorship' while studying and had stayed with her for about a year. I was supposed to remind Jeanne of these days, pay her a visit of courtesy and spend some time with her. Actually my mother had not spent her time in Paris at all well by her own accounting; she now regretted going to too many parties and dances. I was to remind Jeanne of my mother's warm feelings of affection for her and ask if she could show me Paris a little. Since my mother's interests in life had become more and more religious once as she got older and since the woman I was to visit was if anything even more devout than she had been when my mother stayed with her, my time in Paris with Jeanne consisted mainly in visits to well-known religious buildings and institutions. We saw the Madeleine, the society church; and then the famous St. Sulpice for its pedagogical value. The high point of our tour was Institut Catholique, where we viewed the embalmed and sainted body of Catherine Labouré, a 19th-century nun whom the Virgin Mary appeared to and entrusted with the task of spreading devotion to a new cult called the Miraculous Medal. I later learned with interest that the Institut building had once been a Franciscan convent; Danton had met with Marat and Desmoulins there to found the historical Club des Cordeliers in 1790. What was the connection then between these dissimilar worlds? It seemed to me strange that two such non-tangent ideologies should have shared the same material structure, and I have often speculated on the coincidence since then. Waxy, now artificial-looking Catherine had slept away her life without a thought for the revolution that preceded her, nor for those that kept pace with her triumphant ascent to sanctity, nor indeed for those revolutions of the present or the time to come, when realities are made from things she only could dream — lost in her world of abstract hopes, empty illusions. She remains today a caution on the subject of utopian thinking.

And yet. What was it Fred said so prosaically in the last conference? It was one of the remarks the student jots down quickly with the feeling that it 'explains everything' — a sudden brilliant solution to the structural problems of your life. And then when you go back to it and read it again, you wonder. How could you have thought that, wasn't it just a platitude? — like the mystic intuitions and 'oceanic feelings' people used to have on LSD. What do they amount to? Still 'you have to use words,' as a poet I admire once said. I'll repeat Fred's remark for what it's worth with the hope it will make a slightly different comment this time on the Catherine Labouré anecdote. Following Althusser — I think! but I'm no expert here — Fred claims ideology always has a value in itself. And that's because it's always two things at once, a 'false consciousness' and the consciousness of a group. I used to think the moral of that was — nothing's ever lost. But now I think it means something more practical — that all of history refers to our own time.

Well. And I do think of the body of Catherine Labouré as exemplary. It's strange! — that the heritage of revolutionary practice can go rigid and still, putting on the trappings of mortuary art. It's a relationship recalling Lenin's tomb as a specularity facing in two directions, and it refers us back again to the problem of 'apparatuses.' It brings us to the summer institute.

It's curious we didn't see any movies of burials that summer. The Cuban films? — all of them courtesy of Ileana, and all more or less propaganda. We didn't see 'Death of a Bureaucrat' with its open coffins and slapstick comedy routines. But really, who missed its middle-class vulgarity, Havana imitating Paris imitating Hollywood, outworn pastiches from the past? The films we did see weren't so trivial, so frivolous. What they claimed to be was what they were — explanations of things. Certainly the best of them was the classic 'The Other Francisco.' After that they started going downhill a little, and this was sad because there had been so much promise. And in that, it reminds me of my relations with Ileana herself. Caught in our respective apparatuses, the difficulties we had weren't of our private making. We simply had different loyalties and so were at cross purposes. She had her party affiliation, I had my vision of gay politics — and they didn't match. They still don't, and that's a part of the reason I'm writing this narrative. Still, I liked Ileana for a lot of reasons, and in other circumstances we could have been friends.

Let me say a word about what I now call the 'sign of the bat' in these movies — a sort of discourse about exploitation you might say, but truly, a discourse of resistance as well. All this makes me think of Ileana, who is probably organizing teaching brigades this very moment in Nicaragua. How to explain this? I want to get at and untangle the confusions Ileana and I experienced when we met; and indirectly say why, when we met at all, it was polemically. Let me start with the bat marks. Did you know that 'vampire' is not really a Latin American word? Not by origin at least. I think it's interesting that like the word, the legend is really European. This is the sort of thing I learned from Ileana, though she learned it in turn from reading an explanation of this from the brilliant Jean Franco.

I bring up this lore because it's an example of the dream, or 'myth,' as a limit case, just another way of explaining things. And frankly, I thought it was by way of illustrating this that Ileana organized her lectures around the idea of the cannibal. This was the European term for the native tribe encountered by Columbus — the Caribs. They were later reported in the journal of this dubious agent of the kings of Spain to be possessed of certain 'remarkable attributes.' According to the ocular witnesses, they were notably tall and slender in form, and of 'composite nature.' It is claimed that the Caribs are half canine, having, strangely, dogs' heads instead of human ones. Moreover, the witnesses continue, they are known eaters of human flesh — their normal dietary protocol. The entry ends at this point. Naturally the Europeans seized on this idea — a reversal of the facts! — to confer on it a central place of honor in the literatures of their period. The Europeans' discourse of illegitimacy thus attempted to disavow all responsibility for the crime that was actually taking place — a systematic exploitation of the bodies of non-whites for the benefit of the 'civilized' whites at home. Thus in English cannibal and Caliban come to mean the same thing. But here history's cruelty is doubled. After Columbus's infamous errors the writers of Latin American countries can spend almost three centuries writing, as a specialized part of tradition now, to show ghosts of former masters they never were ... cannibals, though Caribs to be sure. Cuba, cannibal, Caribbean, Caliban — words with associations to articulate objective history. Who or what could better pose the question of rhetoric's uses.

Inseparable from this question of rhetoric is history, as our example of the Caribs has shown. One way of describing can be seen to triumph over another. And it's not at all a question of keeping your hands clean — for anyone. Least of all for the historiographers, for the storytellers. How many of us whose function is to describe things have accepted such a characterization? Do we wish that our writing function could be free of its minatory qualities? Those holding the narrative office may accept its radical-negative implications only reluctantly. Each new description of things becomes a challenge to all the old ones, actively seeking to displace them, becoming new ways of seeing things. Contrary to the conventions then, writing is by nature a combative calling. New writings particularly are placed in opposition to old writings, and writings of groups newly coming to power contest vigorously the writings of the groups already in social dominance. But as a writing comes to be established, it comes to take on positive values. It sees itself as less contestatory than it actually is and it disavows its polemic origins. Its estimation of itself is as a maintainer of the status quo, and history comes to have less and less meaning for it. Time no longer seems to be change. The French social philosopher Guy Debord presents evidence of such a mentality in antiquity. 'Those for whom irreversible time has ever existed,' he asserts, 'find in this same time both the memorable and the threat of oblivion: "Herodotus of Halicarnassus presents here the results of his investigations, in order that time not abolish the works of men . . ."' What a disturbing mentality clothes itself in such sentences! *Not* to abolish the works of humankind — a strange way of putting it, I agree, a way of looking at things that would dissolve human conflict in human integration. In this extremity and with shared indignation I feel brotherly feelings toward Ileana — who remains for me the type of those emotions. Isn't the court of last instance always a determining one? The point of view of this century vs. the last for instance. Writers may or may not be part of some oppressed group, may or may not be part of a group that allies itself with groups that are oppressed — but write finally in their own interests. If those interests could somehow not be material, or if our intentions in writing could fail ever to be polemical, who would submit to the pain of joining words together? Writers get their hands dirty, they're culpable. Isn't it pointless to claim innocent intentions? No one cares; and they do not want you to keep on writing.

This leads me to two other David anecdotes, though the first should actually be considered Peter's. I remember that he told it to me on Castro Street one Friday night when we were walking together and looking at the new styles and just plain gossiping about everybody we knew. Somehow stories about love and stories about clothes got all mixed up. Peter was telling me that recently he had started going to the Party educationals along with David and how much everybody seemed to learn. These educationals were just what their name implied and maybe even more so, since the club in Toronto that David was involved with consisted of professors and graduate students mostly. In telling me this Peter followed a train of associations that was purposeful — but only indirectly so. It was structured according to some principle only vaguely guessed at. The Party educational reminded Peter for instance that it was inevitably when he and David were stoned on acid that the same professor, an eccentric CP colleague of his, would come to the door — always at midnight too, because he stayed up late studying — and start those long-rambling, multiple-level monologues about everyone they knew in local politics, with great intelligence and high wit. Peter's sense of irony would point out that this particular colleague always wore shiny suits that never fit and invariably had dandruff on the collar. The suits were 'right off the rack' as Peter put it in his discreet French-Marxist way, with perhaps equal admixtures of a 'grand seigneur' and his own mother, I believe. Peter's sense of humor thus made quite a contrast with David's. Or perhaps I could put it this way — in spite of a surface love of detail and of rich textures, Peter remains at heart a tidy person, I think, and an orderly one. David on the other hand is not. Perhaps it is for this reason that Peter is quite capable of lame jokes, and inept at sarcasm. His humor is actually a form of enthusiasm, great, vague, boundlessly cheerful and unmotivated. In its own polite way, I think, David's humor is more like mine

— melancholy, given to sharpness from time to time, and tendential to its purposes. Which are what? — you might ask. I can't speak for David, and I won't see him again till next summer. but on my own behalf I can say that when I'm joking I usually have in mind a sense of fear or anxiety, and the point of my joking is to elicit a similar anxiety from others by way of comfort. This may be just wishful thinking but it makes me feel restful — I feel it's hygienic. I'd like you to reconsider an incident I mentioned earlier — David's comments in form of a popular song that night when he sang 'It's My Party (And I'll Cry If I Want To).' The second line goes — 'You would cry too if it happened to you.' Funny, of course. But was there a critique of his own party there? Or maybe all of them. I'm not really sure what David meant, and though it's probable he intended these interpretations, who would assert it? There's no law against humming a tune. In any case I'd have wanted to ask Robbie what he thought, though he might not have wanted to venture an opinion, given his own affiliation and ideas on party organization at that time. It's lines of questioning like this that lead you to troubled waters.

The second anecdote expands a little on the point. You could say it's about style, and here once again David comes in. It was David who first taught me to read Jessica Mitford, who, he said, 'put things in an interesting way.' This was on the walk when David told me interesting stories about party cultural life and we discussed funerals. So that may be a further connection — her early book on funerals. The first book may even have brought up the second, though I admit I'm speculating here. In any event I was disposed to like Mitford and her other book on account of another friend who also told me stories about it and her. They related to a time when she had been Mitford's 'writing assistant,' as she said. This evidently involved going over to Oakland and doing research with Mitford. There was a lot of just chit-chat, she said, working and talking together, you know? And that made the time pass easily. That is why, she explained, she wasn't a 'secretary,' as I had suggested. So when I thought about this for a while I saw that their relationship just wasn't that 'official' or business-like, and that sense of sociality seemed very pleasing. That is also why I liked Mitford's book. It was, as they say, 'compassionate and witty' — the account of her life in the Party in the '50s and early '60s. It was everything David said it would be. Her dedication and commitment were so obvious she really didn't have to spell out things. She assumed needs for kindness and good sense while creating gratifying social ties in the comradely struggle to change things, to remake the world. In a similar way I listened to Robbie's stories of seven years of activities in his own organization. And that seemed to give him something in common with David.

'Lifeitselfmanship.' That was the strange name of the little pamphlet Mitford has reprinted in the back of her book. It was a kind of satire on her sister Nancy Mitford's earlier book, the one on 'U' and 'non-U' speech. In it Nancy had made up sample word lists, to tell the two groups apart. Upper-class people in England were supposed to say things like — rich, napkin and false teeth. They were blunt. Middle-class speakers on the other hand were euphemistic and therefore vulgar. They would say things like — wealthy, serviette, and dentures. That was the general idea. Jessica Mitford applied her sister's idea to Party speech. People could be categorized as either 'L' or 'non-L,' Left or non-Left. Here is one of her examples. Non-Left speech — 'Time will tell whether *that plan was OK*.' Left speech — 'The *correctness* of that policy will be *tested in life itself* (Alt. in the crucible of struggle)'. Jessica's viewpoint is more generous than her sister's because she credits her opponents with genuine virtues. Non-Party speakers should be emulated for their plain speech. Nancy's idea by contrast is self-congratulatory. The plainness of the speech of the English ruling class, form her standpoint, gave it ties with heroic feudalism, the military aristocracy of the past. An elitist argument, Nancy's point of view supposes that rich, titled people have some real justification for their privileges and money. Her sister Jessica's viewpoint is very different. On the one hand she is opposed to leftists being fussy or pretentious in their language, but she never denies this language, in spite of itself, a final truth. There is something objective behind it. In one way or another the Storms over Asia, the Locomotives of History and the Life Itselfs testify to something actual, real. That is what I believe, and what I think Mitford believes, and what I hope my readers believe. Words are redeemed by the commitment of a life. They can only be judged by the acts coming from them. If you could look at a person's words by themselves they might or might not tell you very much, since we rarely say what we mean completely and adequately. In the meantime we keep going back to trivialities and banalities, wearing away the only life we have. Of course there are such things as the lives of heroes and their generous, exemplary deaths; yet those heroes remain questionably consoled, seeing themselves so. Those who watch are admirers, and they stand in a majority distance.

Gossip and truth. Truth and rhetoric. How these do a little flip-flop for good and evil. The way they create — and empty — community. The way political people gossip — continually, incessantly — never letting up. it becomes a general fabric in people's lives. It's necessary and constitutive. 'Did you see the smirk on his face when the Spartacist speaker said . . .' (invidiously). 'Of course he never paid her the alimony, do you think a Stalinist would bother about questions of principle . . . ?' Often a false consciousness, but the language of a group too. For the time being, that's the way I'd like to leave it.

I'd like to tell you a little about ideology now — or rather, my ideas on the subject — by telling you about my past, about the time of my first realizations on this peculiar function of language. This all happened during the time I spent in the novitiate of a religious order. Its high point — which summoned up the time for me and gave it meaning — was the funeral of a young classmate named Brother Leo.

Brother Leo's funeral. It's almost an example of ideology getting out of hand. In sheer bulk there was so much of it, of both right and wrong kinds. I have the most pleasant memories of this time of my life — but I do hope to be able to be critical about it when criticism's called for. Brother Leo's funeral and the events that followed it became one of those rich associative nexuses of a past you tend to return to — though with perceptions that get altered as new layers keep on being added — to think through the structural problems of your life. And reading between these lines I hope to find some continuities — ideas, you can't help but hope, that have gotten more human by becoming more historical. The religious communities of my past, I think, stand for political communities in my present, and these in turn for a community of the future that exists only in dreams.

Then it was another story. I defended myself against the obvious inadequacies of those years with the blunt weapons of negativity. The excitements of cynicism and adolescent sarcasm took hold of me, the pleasures of ideological combat drew me on. Severe with myself as with others, my recourse in the inevitable defeat of those years was to the heady satisfactions of technical language — which substituted for sexuality. It was all this, I believe, that brought Sean and me together then and made us determined allies as well as friends.

Ours, you could say, was a romantic point of view, a cynicism of the left. But there were others, jaded, who viewed our religious politics in more worldly fashion as a lot of 'prêchi-prêcha' — as the French brothers from the Motherhouse in Rome called our idealism. They were of the party that called for expediency under the guise of *Realpolitik*. Sean and I were sure we saw through this. We became friends, I think, out of mutual regard for each other's critical powers. Remember Brecht's little song? — 'If there's any stepping to be done, I'll do it!' We were not to be taken in, not by anyone. The curious thing was, though, that we remained believers — devout as the most extreme. The perception of this was always disturbing for me, a vague rustling somewhere at the edges of my consciousness. It made me consider the possibility that I might be making an error, a serious mistake.

I really love my novitiate stories. Who wouldn't want to talk about the colorful aspects of their life, promote themselves, give themselves out as interesting? On the other hand it's so middle-aged and middle-class a thing to do I remain ashamed of myself — so pleasantly egotistical. And yet . . . at a point in their middle years people start sorting out their stories in groups, in an attempt to make their lives more comprehensible to themselves; and the time I spent at Mt. LaSalle has become a nexus or cluster of this kind for me. Recently I've started using these stories to try to center or sift through certain feelings I've had about other men and my relations with them. That is how I justify this endeavor to you. But why not admit the truth? Ultimately my commentaries are fabricated, with the purpose of getting you to like stories I already enjoy telling.

Now as for Leo's funeral that I began telling you about — the important thing is that Sean was rather cruel about this event, though not without reason, as I'll soon explain. My cynicism didn't match his; and he was candid in his opinion. He attributes Leo's death to a deliberate lack of early medical care. Who knows? But the opinion was considered shocking by the other novices, and by myself as well. In my view the awful thing about Sean's opinion was the supposition it made of certain . . . discrepancies . . . between material realities and our ways of speaking, between seeing the obvious and reporting it.

And in the case of Brother Leo's death Sean's opinion seemed particularly disturbing. While we convened for special novenas in chapel and numerous little grace-procuring supplications and visits throughout the day, Brother Leo remained upstairs in his second floor room, alone and dying of cancer. An unpleasant situation, to be sure; recognized as such on all sides. The general idea was that Leo's disease could be arrested by entreaties to the Servant of God Brother Joseph, a 19th century brother from Québec and the order's newest candidate for sainthood. That at least is the way it was explained to us novices. Cynics like Sean pointed out that the order couldn't lose by such a course of action. Live or die, you have your saint. If your prayers are successful, you claim a miracle — and you attribute it to the good graces of Brother Joseph from the Québec province of the order. And if your prayers aren't successful? Then one is consoled by hopes of favors from a new member of the order now in repose above. Double-talk? Yes. But does that mean a person knows what conclusions to draw?

When Leo finally died, everyone wondered where to put him. For the other novices he was just an 18 year old kid out of high school so naturally his family gets to have him back and bury him, right? How could anyone figure it differently? Well, they did — the 'anyone' in this case being the order. The order had gone to a lot of trouble for Brother Leo. It had gotten a special dispensation for him from Rome so that, on account of the advanced course of his disease, he could make his final profession of vows earlier than was prescribed. From the canonical point of view this made Leo a professed brother with his final vows. And this meant he would be buried in the religious habit — which is where the problem started developing. Since Leo's family in southern California naturally wanted their son back for a burial, it was decided that first there would be a family funeral in Los Angeles in the barrio and then the body would get shipped back to the Mount up north for a proper religious ceremony. You can see the situation was a delicate one and could easily have developed into a rather nasty quarrel, with the family on one side and the order on the other side, squabbling over a corpse. Fortunately everybody thought the solution proposed was a good one. Embarrassments would be obviated, and there wouldn't be any problems.

Well, the hitch proved to be the time factor. Consider the situation objectively. Two funerals, one following the other at an interval of two, three days, and the body being shipped over several hundred miles in each direction for each of the services. Plus it was midsummer. And whatever they has already done to him in L.A., he was worse for the wear by the time he got back to the Mount. He was waxy, purplish and bloated up ominously. When they got him onto the catafalque in the middle of the brothers' chapel, I recall there being some whispering as to whether they would strap him down, it all having to do with rigor mortis one supposed. That night we took turns in twos and threes keeping our vigil in chapel, with Sean and me being stuck with the worst slot of all, the 3 A.M. to 4 A.M. watch. It occurs to me to wonder though — was it Sean I was with that night? Uncharacteristically, whoever it was didn't show till around a quarter to. My conclusion is, it wasn't Sean — who would have been punctual given the circumstances. Well, imagine my feelings. I was going to have to be alone in an overheated chapel with a dead person for an hour. And there wasn't any way to avoid this.

It's funny in retrospect, though not at the time, that for my spiritual reading I had chosen an existentialist meditation by Karl Rahner called *The Theology of Death*. Not a happy choice — and the last thing I needed at that point. The chapel was looking really lurid that night, sort of bluish and weird from the fluorescent lights behind the statue niches at the side altars. I haven't any idea why they decided to turn on the fluorescent lights at the side that night and not the main lights. Obviously no one was thinking about saving money because the furnace was on too, and going full blast; so I don't think that was the reason. The bluish light made everything look morbid and creepy. And aren't things unhealthy enough as it is? — I wondered rather idly. Carrying out this thought, I wondered if I shouldn't apply it to my vocation, re-examine the rationality of my life-calling. I asked myself if the whole idea of Spanish Baroque and its religion wasn't in fact rather unhealthy. And isn't chastity pretty unhealthy too? And death — isn't that the most unhealthy thing of all! But unbeknownst to my conscious self, my meditations were taking me in a direction that proved to be quite blameless and orthodox. I decided that all the provocations of life, including death, should be considered beneficial, since they were but a part of life; and I concluded that ascetical theology was built on common sense. I vowed to faithfully read a page of the Imitation of Christ in the morning and then again in the evening before bed.

Meanwhile Leo quietly lay there, looking iridescent and satiny and ghastly. I was sure he was going to burst his straps and sit up. I imagined him seeing we were all alone in the church and then taking revenge — for all the bad things I had ever said about him. And I saw exactly how he would look, all bloody and black with horrible matted hair, and one eye swollen closed and the other staring straight ahead like he was crazy. It was really awful to think about. All he had to do was roll one leg over the edge of his coffin, and that would be the end of me. And I realized that dead people are quite deceptive that way. Naturally you imagine that they would be slow and awkward, and extremely clumsy in their movements. But one only has to think twice to realize the truth. In fact their accumulated resentments and treacheries give them enormous potentials of energy. And a person would be a fool not to think that eventually they will put this energy to a 'practical' use. In short one may assume the worst. No point in being superstitious, I thought, yet all the same, you've got to look after number one, nobody else is going to do it for you. And on that prudential thought I spent the remaining time of a very uncomfortable watch.

And the next day wasn't all that much better either, though it was supposed to be. According to the theology anyway, a mass of the dead is a happy occasion. The words of the liturgy promise that the dead will rise again, and that the remains of a human being that you see will somehow magically come together again at the end of the world. But that promise turns out to seem awfully vulgar when you actually look at a dead body. They're just a thing now and not a person and if you have any sense in you, you can see that they never will be a person again. They're just a dumb mess! — and the dead person in front of us looked awfully dead. The funeral mass was definitely taking an emotional toll on Leo's relatives. Half way through the Dies Irae an elderly woman dressed in black stood bolt upright and broke away from the relatives who were trying to hold her back. It was a distressing scene of course, but what was she going to do? She began screaming and waving her arms but surprisingly none of the relatives seemed concerned. When she got up to the coffin she stopped, and with dignity slowly bent down to the blackened corpse and kissed it. It was impossible not to feel a beautiful rightness in her gesture. But on the other hand — kissing a dead body! — a corpse that had started to decompose some time ago, days even. My thoughts of the previous evening came back to me with full force. Was death itself a contamination? Or was it the dead body that contaminated you? And if there wasn't any contamination at all, why were the theologians so anxious to prove that the deceased was now 'with God.' It was obvious that something was wrong. Maybe it was from some misguided sense of compassion, but didn't religion encourage people to be crazy? But why did people have to be crazy at all, I wondered. I thought there was some cheating going on here. Only it wasn't clear to me for whose benefit this was all taking place.

The craziness continued for a whole day. After the funeral mass we went up to the little graveyard in back of us to put Leo in his plot. There was a procession up the hill and then we gathered around the open grave while the priest sang about the angels taking Leo's soul to paradise. The priest sprinkled the thing we carried and we all said good-bye in our hearts. That was all there was. We turned to go back and two groundskeepers were left there to cover him up. When we arrived at the novices' courtyard, the community brothers left us to have refreshments. One of the older brothers told us we could have the rest of the day off up to the evening prayer. We could do what we wanted, he said, so long as we were back for compline. After that I remember having a sort of blank heavy feeling like overeating. The afternoon looked rather purposeless. I guess I looked as bad as I felt because when Sean glanced at me over his shoulder, I hardly grimaced in return. Coming over to my side and griping my arm sanctimoniously, Sean boomed out his voice in such a hearty way I couldn't resist smiling. 'Would you

care to join me in a couple of bottles of wine in the bell tower, brother?'
I would and I did. We needed the diversion, and an afternoon of alco-
holic sarcasm seemed the only way we would make it through the day
till compline. Once in the bell tower Sean told me some sexist stories
about an aunt who had been a witch, a bruja — she didn't speak much
English. He mimicked the way she talked. Sean said she was always
at the botica and got potions and such and supposedly did something
to Unca John once but he wouldn't talk about it because he was afraid
of her. He liked to swagger when he talked like this and I liked to
watch him. He only bragged when he felt comfortable. Then he told
me about all the girls he used to make love to. He said it was like a
drug and that once you started you couldn't stop. That was why Unca
John was the way he was, he had been a priest once but he couldn't
take all the tension that built up from his vow of chastity. It keeps
building up and then one day something just snaps, Sean explained.
He snapped his fingers by way of illustration. I was really amused,
but also impressed. I knew he was being witty but was a little uncer-
tain about how serious he was. It was like when he told me about the
cholo gangs he had been in and their exploits in doing this and that
against other groups — I never knew how much to believe him, he
could have been making it all up. But then he continued. Sometimes
the pressure gets to be too much — he paused darkly. What can you
do? — he asked. You give in, don't you? I nodded with what I hoped
was sophistication and tried not to feel uneasy. Was I failing to understand something? I looked at Sean to try to read something on his features. His face was completely expressionless, and he was already on
to still another example. He told me that when he went out for group
walks in the afternoon he sometimes felt like he was being pulled

apart. Ideas would come into his head and he wasn't able to keep them out. Sometimes even trees and bushes just seemed like good places for fucking. He could imagine having sex with his girlfriends all over. And the thought would come up that in the end he would pay for all this — by going crazy. Somehow the expression of this last sentiment alarmed me more than anything else, though I didn't know why, and I hastily agreed that this all must be quite difficult for him. All I knew was that I was by now quite uncomfortable. Our conversation seemed to have a drift to it that I couldn't quite grasp, some added meaning that I was failing to understand.

I have to admit that I was awfully dumb, or else Sean was. But in light of what Nick was to tell me later, I'll tell you right now, that latter possibility just wasn't too likely. My supposition is this — absolutely *nothing*, short of direct physical action, could have gotten through to me. Alas! In order for me to have understood the meaning of my conversation with Sean, I would, unfortunately, have had first to admit that I was as sexual a human being as the next person; and that is something I could not have done then. The possibility of sex seemed exactly the same as the possibility of death. The sequence of rigorous logic suggested this — if a person is once prevailed on to have sex, doesn't it follow that they may also be prevailed on to die? The prudent person therefore is wary of beginning what may not be concluded. And from this point of view — as I admit only too sadly now — the corpse we had just finished burying was an object lesson as much as a dead person. It's a mistake to trust in physical satisfactions. In the end they come to nothing. Yet there remained an important fact in all this that had escaped my notice. However ill-advised a course of action it may be, people continue to die. And that is what happens whether you like it or not, it's not a correctable error. Should I confess what is probably only too obvious? In those salad years of my Catholic Cartesianism I was still a young colt, frisky and heady with newly tasted pleasures of thought and I yearned — oh how I yearned! — to be free in the vast springtime fields of the Idea, chewing and chomping where I would. The world for me was shot through with the green flames of reason, and even in my religious vocation in life — no, *especially* there! — why shouldn't those forms manifest themselves? As far as I was concerned, the opposite of ideas meant obscurantism, not friendship or community — as I would call them now. That reason and community might in some way be in dispute was a possibility that never suggested itself to my innocent consciousness. Reason for me was an improvement scheme, a practical global betterment system — a combine in which, as it happened, I held common stock. There wasn't an argument I could think of for not believing that a religious community couldn't be like everything else in contemporary America. It could be as modern and up-to-date as Betty Furness opening her refrigerator. Nobody ever told me this wasn't possible. And when they did, I was out of our community and embarked on another life.

Bur while I was there I knew what I liked and loved against my better principles, and I understood what I loved through the emotions. My affective life taught me to value the shapes of collectivity I saw there, which formed alienated but actual ideals of friendship and community. It was a promise of things to come. At our robing ceremony we were filled with exhilaration. The collectivity was already beginning. As the novices filed out to make their vows in front of the family and friends who had come to watch, each of the older brothers would come up one by one to welcome us. Then each of the older ones would kiss each of the younger ones, till everyone was embraced by everyone — visibly signifying the festival of unity and love. It was a community structured like a narration, and its meaning was an exchange of certain signs — a patterned exchange, rather than an anarchic one. Love, I found out, was not the same thing as spontaneity.

What might be called the business end of this community ordering process was another religious exercise — called chapter of faults. The chapter made sure that love didn't compromise unity. As the privileged exercise of communal reconstitution in fraternal correction, chapter of faults thus stood out unmistakably as the principal disciplinary function of the community. A river needs its bed or course, as was explained to us, or how does it flow? If love isn't orderly, it isn't love at all! Well, it was an attractive argument. Too attractive as a matter of fact — and Sean and I decided that the exercise really should be opposed. Religious life wasn't particularly democratic as it was, and chapter of faults seemed only too likely to appeal to the kookier and more suspect sides of people who took up religious life. It remained an unworkable relic from another age.

Politics exacerbated the matter. Sean and I had aligned ourselves with the liberal-progressive faction at the novitiate, and our stance on the authoritarian chapter meeting was interpreted as a radical-liberal 'pushiness,' with polarizing overtones. Conservative novices repeated about us the historical charge once made about the Port-Royalist Jansenists — 'Purer than angels but prouder than devils.' I never found this attempted witticism very funny; but for some reason it always sent Sean into gales of laughter. And this tactic took our conservative brothers by surprise. They had assumed we would make a counter-charge, presumably also in a spirit of 'wit,' and that their cut-rate erudition would then carry the day. So it disturbed them that Sean didn't bother to reply. With a wonderful hearty indifference he stood there daring them to do their worst, braving all their doctrinal fusillades — a free-thinking Gulliver among the traditionalist Lilliputians. As for myself, though, the matter was more complex. Somewhere inside of me I wondered if our enemies' charges didn't have some secret truthfulness to them. Nagged by doubts about our course of action, I wondered if there was a place for dissent in community life. Could there licitly be a difference between 'public' and 'private' in community life — and didn't the possibility of disagreement presuppose such a difference? Perhaps when you joined a community, it was exactly this that you had to give up, important as it seemed. Our opponents charged us with being divisive of community life — an accusation of some seriousness as far as I was concerned. But on the other hand, the chapter embodied elements that were extremely disruptive of community life — it was both manipulative and authoritarian. It was a medieval holdover that deformed community life. And as for the charge that we were disruptive of genuine traditions, how, I wondered, could you expect anyone to defend those traditions when they have become only gestures — the artifacts of museums?

Naturally in my novitiate days my questions didn't have the explicitness I'm giving them now. I was led on in fact by my emotions, my affective life. I admitted we weren't like the Carmelites who used whips and slept on pallets, who observed the letter of the old rules, but I thought our disciplinary practices were at least odd and at times a little disgusting. When I thought of practices like our chapter of faults I felt as if there weren't cars any more or TVs, as if when you went outside, supermarkets would have ceased to exist, and there would be disease and plague and misery. Coarse men would be beating animals pulling dirty wooden carts, and they would be burning people at the stake. I imagined people poisoning their neighbors' wells, and cows growing sick mysteriously, and crippled people or old people or foreigners being stoned to death. This possibility alarmed us, and we resolved to act. Sean and I would become defenders of freedom and of humanitarian reason. That was our rhetoric. But did we realize that in becoming defenders of reason we also became foes of Power? I'm not sure I can say. All I know is that we crossed a line. On the other side of that line we discovered we had set ourselves up against authority.

How did it all come to a head? I'll tell you. But first a word about the actual mechanics of the chapter meetings. This is the way they worked. After the noon prayer we gathered in the common room and knelt beside our desks. Then following a brief opening prayer for guidance in this exercise, the director would tap his large desk from the back of the room, as a signal for the procedure to begin. The first novice from the first row would now go up front — the first victim! Then you'd kneel on a low platform, gazing fervently all the while at the wounded corpus of the crucifix in front of you and begin reciting the formulas prescribed by our Rules and Constitutions. 'My very dear brothers,' you would recite — in awkward translation of the rule book's French *mes très chers frères* — 'I humbly beg your pardon for the following faults.' And you would name them, eyes fixed on the crucifix of the dying Jesus. You would list your infractions of the week, going into details to the extent that your piety urged you. And it was here that Sean and I always started to get uneasy — the transparent appeal to masochism really disturbed us. Then there was the political dimension of all this. There was a principle involved here for us. God was, for us, an abstraction. An important one to be sure, but an abstraction nonetheless. So we didn't really have any strong objections to accepting His corrections, which were as vague, abstract and non-specific as the divine Nature itself. If God was something like the Ultimate Meaning in Things, who could object to a tip of the hat in that direction — in the direction of Everything That Is? That would have been as senseless as objecting to World History. God was, to put it candidly for you, just not that important. People were. Asking *people's* forgiveness meant submission in a real, actual sense; and it was that that Sean and I just couldn't stand. As a result, Sean and I got the reputation of being Proud. As I look back on things now, we may indeed have been, if not exactly proud, maybe a little stuck-up. But who doesn't cheat — just a teensy bit — when it comes to public confessions? And so at this point the rules prescribed that your brothers jog your memory a bit by pointing out the faults you had somehow overlooked. Naturally there would be a great many of them. Of course no one *had* to criticize anyone else; but naturally too, the pleasure was hard to resist. The victim was encumbered with a sign that announced 'kick me!' So why not? Everyone would end up accusing everyone else — so that there was this marvelous little terroristic control induced, which inevitably worked in favor of the superiors of the community and obviously not for the rank and file novice brothers. Well, Sean and I had had it with all this, and we decided to take a stand. For our part we wouldn't accuse anybody of anything.

We got away with it for a while, but as chapter followed chapter and the weeks went by, our non-participation became evident. Our silence became marked as Defiance — a rebellion that had to meet with comeuppance. But when Authority struck, it struck with a milky mildness and bureaucratic vagueness that disconcerted us. The Director called us into his office and gave us an exasperatingly mature lecture. He explained that our abstention from the chapter exercise was creating ill-will and dissension in the community. Why were we doing this? Did we enjoy dividing the community? Now it was true that our chapter wasn't a terribly democratic thing but it was a ancient tradition and, as we surely realized, one particularly recommended by the Founder, St. LaSalle. So in the future would we *please* be sensible about this whole matter and make an effort? That is, do the Director the favor of making *at least one criticism* at each chapter meeting. We assured him we would. This ostensible compliance of ours was — alas! — grounded in utter bad faith. We intended to misrepresent ourselves and lull the Director into a false feeling of security until we could form a new plan. Following the letter, therefore, but not the spirit of our promise to him, for the next meeting, and then the next, and then the one after that until our right to dissent was firmly established de facto, we criticized . . . each other! — and so continued our grand plan of wrecking the chapter. Our long-suffering Director was too fatigued after that to provoke another confrontation. Did we accomplish anything in this remembered tempest in a pot of clerical tea? Probably. We probably gained something, in spite of adventurism, for individual and human-democratic rights — and for the principle that rules ought to be reasonable and non-authoritarian. But on the other hand somehow we lost something, intangible but as important, something having to do with community values. As it seems now, the point would have been something other entirely — and going beyond these antagonisms to an actual practice. But such a speculation suspends a whole group of real histories.

I find parallels between that situation and the choices that face me now. Though there are differences too, and finally they are more important. Little by little I want to show why and how. For politics is to religion as reality to the dream. So that religious collectivity — expression, not realization of human need — remains important for me as a figure, as metaphor.

I do want to move on now, but I'm not quite sure how to do it. I'm halfway through and see so much meandering in these pages that I want to explain myself before going on. It all has to do with what a 'theme' in writing might be — and wondering if I've strayed from this theme in giving you such a long extract from my novitiate years. My theme probably has most to do with a very strong feeling that telling stories actually has an effect on the world, and that a relation is achieved between the one telling those stories and her or his audience and history. Consequently, it's necessary to be truthful, responsible, and so on. but if you lie in tiny places, you had better be ready to accept the effects that flow from this. Because they will certainly come back to you. Writers who think they can ever get off scot-free will pay for this by becoming superficial people. And then after a while they even stop caring about that. They don't care that they don't *touch* an audience anymore.

Think of the way it used to be. 'Arma virumque.' The goddess coming down to some writer and saying, 'Here's your theme, now write about it!' And he/she does. But if a theme is a relation, certainly everything changes. Let's say these 'themes' become power, friendship, ideology and so on. You want what you write to actually *cause* these to come to exist, you don't want just to describe them. The story is going to be impure; just like real, actual life is, in which these actual qualities exist and are found mixed in the social class and historical period of the audience you are addressing. You can't be an idealist. You must learn to follow certain rhythms — both of yourself and of those with whom you want to speak, and upon whose social and historical trajectories you want to have effects. A certain amount of patience becomes important; and a storyteller has to learn to wait on occasions and implications — and learn, too, to become as polite toward them as toward people. Politeness becomes the preeminent virtue in a writer.

How did I come to think this way? A short time ago I wanted to show how you can use language in certain ways to illuminate and structure the relations people have of their own friendship and love. This at any rate is what I imagined my story was about. I built this narration round a real life incident in which, in an exchange, I told a friend of mine some of the religious stories of my childhood. The story described how we would take these stories apart and then put them together in new ways. I hoped to show in this way how people exchanged affections and linguistic treasures. The story was called *My Walk with Bob*. When I finished it I sent it off to another friend, someone I hadn't seen in a long time.

Time went by. Then one day this other friend called me on the phone, but for another reason. She wanted to chat, really, and told me all about her activities as a girl scout troop leader and mother. I was very happy to hear from her and listened contentedly as she told me about some of her children's new interests and some of her own. We also talked about my friend's mother, whom I remembered visiting several times with my friend when she lived here in the Bay Area. Then my friend mentioned the story I had written. She said she loved it, it was great. I was glad she liked it, her opinion was important. Had her mother read the story and did she like it? She hadn't yet. But my friend was positive her mother would like it very much. There was only one qualification. Her mother was old, my friend reminded me, and she would have to pretend to be shocked for a while on account of the, ah, sexual indiscretions in my story. Naturally, she would make a pretense of being shocked, though those would not be her true feelings. I would only know her true feelings by, say, her way of pouring tea when I visited. Or else, my friend continued, her mother might suddenly bring up the subject of the classics — how she had always enjoyed Dickens and Thackeray, and didn't we also think literature was important in bringing up the young? This would be followed by a knowing smile in my direction — 'and some *contemporary* literature we can all think of too!' My friend's mother expressed herself in her own way, she followed her own rhythms. This imaginative account of my friend's mother's reception of my book pleased me and left me with a wonderful, glowing feeling, which, however I didn't understand for some time.

But this is what I finally understood. My friend's response to my book and her description of her mother's response made me realize the importance I attached to pleasing people when I wrote. Being a good writer is making people like or love you! But then the question is, how do you do that? Well, one way of course — and a rather obvious way — is to make people feel that you are a really good person. Kind, generous, loyal to your friends and so on. Then there is a more sophisticated tack — you appeal to their better natures. You point out the wonderfully charming sides of their own potential virtues. Here is where you bring in politics. You suggest they will be far better and more developed and happy with themselves in life if they will start to be a little political now and then. And then you hope that if they do start getting political, they will thank you for it. They will want to attribute wisdom to you, and esteem you. Yet in the long run, neither of these two tacks goes far enough, I decided, because basically, people are egotists. The truth is, people really want to hear about themselves. And they want pictures of themselves they can recognize. I decided to think of this as a personality 'effect' — a feeling of recognizing people.

I would make images of people in my stories so they would have the pleasure of seeing themselves. With every person named, life would be tangled in the text. I wanted people to feel they had a stake in this writing and credit it and affirm it and give it a community and social life it could only have if *many* people saw their representations there, not just *one* person. Not just myself — since I could now tell about others. Politeness, pleasure, related to people's responses to what you had written. Your text could not begin until people were able to start loving and hating you on account of it. Finally I wanted a text so tangled up with others that it would be their intentions, and not mine, that gave it such place as it would have in a large social history.

And that is what happened. It is how I discovered — quite by accident and from a person who had been absent from my life for a number of years — the real meaning of my earlier relationship with Brother Sean. That person was Nick, who appeared from out of the blue a few years ago and then got lost again. I suppose we'll be in and out of each other's lives indefinitely in no predictable way. But actually, this way of doing things turns out to be quite reassuring, rhythmical, respectful even. If someone asks about friendships like this, I sometimes say it's like being in the army. People often feel close like that, though they can't say why. It's also like political life — in its group basis, it seems to me. If a person works with someone on things they believe in or care about, they form very strong ties with that other person. The ties remain, even if it happens you come no longer to 'believe' in what brought you together. They are still important, and the friendship persists. Ideology, one might say, has been a pretext for discovering friends. It's a very romantic or fateful story, because just as often as not one destiny or fate will supplant another. Or you think you've lost forever some segment of your life or history, and it suddenly returns, new and brilliant! — yet too often, dusky with a sadness you've seen before.

And that is how my relations with Sean appeared — after I saw Nick again. We met, as it happens, quite accidentally, and just as I was getting ready to leave for Minneapolis and the first Summer Institute of the MLG. It was a particularly beautiful morning — and I had just left the hair salon after spending nearly twice as much money as I should have. The idea I had then was that looking nice can be a political act and should be encouraged. But I was feeling guilty nonetheless. $22 for a haircut! This must have seemed an odd way of thinking to Nick because he seemed amused. I was just out of Sassoon's thinking of all the items on my checklist and flying along in a terrific hurry when there he was. There was Nick — smiling at me from out of nowhere, smiling and waving at me from across Market Street. We were awfully happy to see each other. It didn't take long before we had sketched out details from about ten years, both of us noting that we had to decide on new courses in life. Nick was going to cut hair — strange, on the day I went to Sassoon's! — and as for myself, I told Nick, I didn't see how I could still suppose I would be a professor. We talked a little longer and made a date to see each other in a few days.

It was a holiday when I saw Nick the second time, and we went for a leisurely afternoon stroll up Twin Peaks and out to Stern Grove to meet Jonathan and some friends for an outdoor musical performance there. We stopped frequently along the way, taking in the view and allowing each other time and opportunity for thoughts about the ten years we hadn't seen each other. Naturally we talked about Sean. I assumed now, just as I had done in the novitiate, that Sean and I had been special friends — with a particular intimacy Nick hadn't shared. But after leaving the novitiate something had happened which marked a cooling in this relationship, and I wanted to tell Nick about it — since it seemed to show a kind of arrogance or spirit of macho developing in Sean. Nick and I turned out to be gay, and Sean was the one who was straight. Soon after leaving the order he married. A family man, he now had several children.

We had paused at this point and were enjoying the view near the summit where Clarendon Avenue turns down again after the TV tower and continues past a woodland reservoir out toward the Sunset. Curiously, Nick seemed abstracted, and I couldn't see the reason for it. As we looked out at the harbor the bay seemed too blue, the sailboats too white. They looked like pasteboard. I had caught Nick's mood of reverie. It was a private moment for us both, and, I supposed, we were both wrapped in thoughts of days gone by. Isn't it sad, I said to Nick, that we were all so close to each other without being more, well, *intimate*. Then, when Nick made no comment, I elaborated. 'All that time without sex, what a waste!' Nick laughed at this, and I decided to follow up the thought with the story about Sean I had promised him.

The anecdote I told Nick concerned my chance meeting with Sean in the full Counter-Culture days in the so-called Summer of Love of 1967. I had been living with Joel, a mystical ex-New Yorker who previously had done drag but was now just a street person, as he put it, meaning that he lived by selling dope on Haight Street and spending most of his time hanging around in front of the Garuda tea shop, or Metz's Superior Doughnuts, as it was also called. Joel had two acquaintances who in different ways turned out to be quite important for me. The first was Sister Mary, still a nun then but already a poet — and who, according to Joel, would use his flat to change into civilian clothes, smoke dope and temporarily become a street person herself. I'm not sure whether I believe this exactly as Joel told it, but true or not the story added to the generally 'spiritual' atmosphere at Joel's during the time I lived there. Equally interesting to me, and I suppose by most people's reckoning as strange and exotic, was Joel's private guru. I wish I could remember his name, but I can only recall that it was one of those names that will never recur, and in their golden silliness bring back a whole era. It was a name like Bliss Child. Or Neruda or Shambala. A name to make a person smile indulgently at a past that might be one's own; part of history now, filled with gentle walks through the park, the aggressive smells of sandalwood and patchouli and the soughing of eucalyptus trees. When I first met him, Joel's guru was maybe 10 or 11 — at most 12 years old. This didn't surprise me and seemed totally unremarkable to everyone else as well. His parents were mystically inclined adult hippies who, right from the beginning, had raised him in a perfect awareness of his own godhead; and even to skeptics he was an unusual child. Early on he realized that he had been chosen to liberate adults from their timidities and anxieties about themselves, and in particular their sexual fears. For reasons I never wholly understood, it made him unspeakably sad to see adults who were unspontaneous, or worried and always fretting, or otherwise miserable through their own fault. He wanted to cajole them into being like himself; he wanted them to become joyful children again. And though Joel was one of the objects of his ministrations in all this, he was also — as I failed to realize at the time — a co-conspirator.

Joel and his not quite mature guru had gone into the missionary business with the laudable goal of proselytizing among those who needed it most. And their spiritual enterprise had targeted me.

This all became clear to me one day when the child-guru wandered in to join me as I lay watching TV test patterns. Joel was, as it appeared, out of the house — and there I was zonked out from dope-smoking, lying on the low double mattress that served as a couch. A combination of test patterns and strong marijuana made me more or less oblivious to my surrounding, and I hardly noticed when the small guru climbed on up beside me. What did he want? But it didn't really matter to me. I was preoccupied with some new incomprehensible mish-mash of student politics, Eastern mysticism, and Hegelian philosophy. Well. First he untied my shoes. A response? Not at all. So then he climbed up near my chest and started undoing my shirt. I remember hearing him giggle at that point, and I remember not understanding. I was dense and had made little progress in this area since my novitiate days with Brother Sean. But then he started unzipping my pants and then finally I *did* understand. It came to me in a flash, bubbling up to me on the young guru's spiritual laughter, as it were. He wants *sex*, I told myself. I was amazed — filled with consternation — incredulity. How in the world . . . ? Could he really believe that I . . . !? With a determined effort I drew on years of internalized prohibitions and repressed the desire that was awakening in me. Establishing the situation on an ethical basis, I became master of my fate again. 'I am an adult,' I calmly told the young Shambala, 'and you are a child.' Confidently I made my point. 'Don't you see it would be wrong?' But whether Shambala understood the force of my arguments or not at this point was an entirely academic question, for the diminutive guru had advanced to the stage of gurgling little kisses on the mouth. All in vain! He could as well have been kissing a Foster's Frosty Freeze. I had made up my mind and was no longer seducible. I attributed this to strength of character. Would I, you might ask, make this evaluation today? Of course not! I will tell you! A thousand times no! Quite truthfully, the young guru's consciousness, hippie-style and flower child as it was, was in this area far in advance of my own. Besides, what may be material fact to all this, Shambala wouldn't have had much incentive in continuing a seduction so slightly appreciated. In any case with the crisis now past, we settled back with a wonderful comradely freedom to watch the changing test patterns. I ask the reader to note the scene well. Has she or he never seen its sweet like in some old book, some foxed gravure or curious vignette and yearned to know its truth? Look again, look again! — beneath these old imaginings. There is no happier couple than we were in that one moment, I promise you. A conclusion? The mildest of the mild. Little Shambala and I drifting off toward fitful sleep, a larger shoulder and head against a sympathetic and smaller one — till Joel would wake us for dinner.

Now I don't remember how it was that Sean came to visit us in our irregular little ménage, but I do recall my own self-fulfilling prophecies that he would be shocked. And shocked he was — he was pensive, morose and clearly uncomfortable. But here I broke off my relation and casually observed to Nick that it was obvious Sean had been alarmed by indications of a gay living arrangement. Since Sean was rigorously anti-sexual in our novitiate days, as I explained to Nick, how could he be expected to be comfortable in this free-and-easy environment? But Nick was mysteriously silent again, and I began to consider how I might critique this strange behavior. But as I look at it now the problem was no more mine than it was Sean's. And no less. It had to do with what I consider a tacit agreement made early on to simply ignore the sexual components in male friendship — an agreement that went with the male bonding of an earlier time. Hadn't we learned in high school to dispense with sex for the sake of a more elevated camaraderie? Friendship! Ideals of mental companionship! I know there was something wrong in all this, but I didn't know what. Even later, how could a serious breach of this rule not seem threatening — to both Sean and me?

And in this sense I think a conflict with Sean was inevitable. One after another I had lost most of my best friends from high school and college this way. The very type of these conflicts was J. — my closest friend from these years. Who could have enjoyed each other's company more than we did? Shared more? Spent more time together? We were a paradigm of friendship, and everything depended on a single assumption — that we didn't touch each other. And if situations — rarely — threatened this assumption, they were soon forgotten. Let me give you an example. J. had given a beer party for old friends from high school in our first summer home from college. We wouldn't room together till later, but we were already best friends. Late in the party when everyone got drunken and disorderly, J. and I were sitting on the floor side by side against the wall of his parents' front room, watching the party's deterioration. Our own intoxication was more an act of bravado than a real state — a pretext for trying to say what we couldn't on other occasions. 'Are you feeling what I'm feeling?' J. asked me, and his leg rubbed mine so I would understand. But I could only dissimulate and answered 'no' for fear of losing face. The loss was mine, since it was an invitation to further friendship not extended again. And soon we had forgotten about the occasion. Years later after our college years and after I had gone through novitiate and graduate school and had begun to meet other gay men, I met J. again. He told me he thought I had changed — I thought he was changed too. His marriage was unsteady, and he felt more or less uncomfortable living in San Francisco. We would drink and he would talk — mostly about the time he had spent on Cyprus in government work — while I listened. J. had never been in the C.I.A. as many of us supposed that P. had. But it seemed to me that the two of them were on one side of an invisible boundary line that our circle of masculine friendships had created — a boundary line I had been warned against crossing, and then crossed. My sexuality seemed to me one more choice of an opposition that was general, one development of many in that era of protests against the war in Viet Nam and a whole oppositional youth culture of the late '60s. More and more J. saw in me, I think, a choice for a disorder that appeared foreign to his own life. We saw each other, but less frequently. Then J. moved away — and we weren't friends anymore.

One by one my old friendships had dissolved this way. When Sean came to visit us at Joel's I feared the same basic mechanism would erode this friendship as well. My open avowal of a sexual personality amounted to a political demand — didn't it? — that other men change their assumed codes of behavior. This is how I explained my fears of Sean's visit to Nick. Most men I knew wouldn't change, I argued, and I didn't see why Sean would be different.

Nick's discretion — or was it loyalty to Sean? — seemed to shy away from the question. 'Oh Brother David!' he said teasingly, using my old religious name. It's a form of playful camp I can't resist, so soon we were on the subject of our novitiate days, gossiping about all the people we had known there. What were they like now? Not many, it turned out, were still in the order. This didn't surprise me, since most of us had been early-college age. Where was Roland? Still in the order? — Strange! He was always the one we thought would leave first. Then Tim. There was a strange one. So competent, enthusiastic — I thought he'd be Provincial some day! An insurance man in the valley now, married and with kids. And Gilbert was working with Cesar Chavez since he left — though that wasn't a surprise since it was what people expected. They always said he was political. I said I had seen in the paper that Brother Gregory died, and there was a new president in the winery. Nick just laughed at this. He knew I disliked the winery. Sean and I were always troublemakers in that area. We were the ones who irritated the Director and the other superiors by talking about winery profits and how they seemed to support the brother president in a very comfortable lifestyle. There was the brand-new Lincoln or Imperial each year. There was the vacation house for entertaining customers and relaxing after a hard week of business. There was the good food and good liquor. And naturally too, the special dispensations from community exercises and the not very demanding religious schedules. These were the perks the brothers in the winery operation very easily seemed to become accustomed to. When the Brother President's limousine would roll up to the novitiate on Sundays, Sean and I would sweetly quote the Scriptures to each other. 'Brother Sean,' I would say to Sean, 'Seek first the kingdom of God.' Then Sean would roll his eyes at the approaching limousine and answer, 'And all things will be added to you.' We were really quite talented at this sort of thing. 'Brother David,' Sean would say, 'Consider the lilies of the field,' — and I would supply the answer, 'They neither spin nor do they weave.' Then Sean would add the final phrase with a rhetorical sweep of the hand in the direction of a well-tailored Brother President just then stepping out of his blue Chrysler Imperial — 'Yet not even Solomon in all his glory was arrayed as one of these.' When the Brother President looked over in our direction to smile hello — we'd show our teeth and smile right back. We sincerely hoped to be just as phony as he was for the occasion. Good boys! — And he'd wave absentmindedly. Or else we would just quote the sub-director at his most cynical, giving us reasons for staying in the order. 'After all,' he'd tell us with a coarse wink of complicity, 'it's three squares and a bed . . .' But the irony in all this, as Nick proceeded to point out, was that Sean's lifestyle these days was not exactly ascetic these days. He had a beautiful house, probably worth over $100,000, a comfortable job and — probably most important of all — a more secure berth in life than he would have had if he had stayed in the order. Was I a little shocked at hearing this? No — but I pretended to be. I wanted Nick to continue talking about Sean, in whom we both maintained an interest.

It was Nick rather than myself who over the years remained close to Sean. I told Nick I was sorry for this — I wished Sean and I had stayed closer than we did. It suddenly occurred to me as I was making protestations that I might well have been misinterpreting Nick's odd behavior all along — his mysterious silence and refusal to comment on my anecdotes about Sean. What if, I wondered — just what if . . . Nick's relationship with Sean was deeper and more 'serious' than my own had been? Fifteen years had passed since we had been novices together. Was it possible I remembered things selectively? — or that I was even just plain wrong! The possibility alarmed me, and with growing self-doubt I looked over at Nick — as if for some explanation.

Nick didn't seem to be overly concerned with my distress at this point. He returned our conversation to my account of Sean's visit during the Summer of Love. He said that Sean's behavior then, while maybe a little impolite, couldn't possibly be considered sexist — or homophobic. And why not? Nick's answer astounded me — 'Because during the whole time we were in the novitiate Sean and I were sleeping together.'

I considered the implications of Nick's announcement. In a flash I realized I had been making some fundamental error in evaluating this period of my life — the whole decade of my twenties. Even after becoming more of a 'sexual' person myself I continued to suppose that no one else had made any more progress than I had in resolving the split between sexuality and friendship — a split that seemed general in the lives of most men. I looked at Nick with wonder and a new respect for 'laws of unequal development.' Could it really be true then . . . ? Nick was serenely blessing me with his smile. Yes, unquestionably. Seeing Nick's sweet and ingenuous smile I knew that everything he had said was indisputably, undeniably true. And it made sense out of a whole period in my life when I refused to see what was there in front of my eyes.

Men have real problems, all of us. When we get into a political situation you would think we would change. But no. Years of bad training are just not erased with a set of propositions. Things don't happen that way. Maybe political men have some of the worst of these problems. But when I say them, don't I mean us? Of course I do — most of the time — why wouldn't I? My reluctance would be guided by marginal cases. These are negligible for most purposes, but — wouldn't you admit it yourselves? — still useful in reaching limits. It's not difficult for me to imagine, say, a type of man, a *straight* man I will say, with laments, sighs and weeping perched like Job on a hill of detritus that may also be called 'trash heap of history' — cursing the day he was born! Oh, a *type* mind you — and not all, to be sure. And yet. Sad case piles on sad case; example follows implacable example. What discouragement is there for us here! Allegiances strain, and at last you're driven to it. 'There's structural difficulty' — you say — 'and it's time to change!'

It was with such thoughts that I left for my Summer Institute a few short weeks after seeing Nick. The day I got there, I pinned to my t-shirt a little pink triangle I had been wearing through most of the summer. I wore it for homosexuals killed in the German concentration camps and for a gay man named Robert Hillsborough, killed earlier that year in San Francisco by a group of youths shouting anti-gay slogans. When people would ask who Robert Hillsborough was, I would explain. I would also explain the inverted pink triangle — an identity badge for gays in Nazi extermination camps. All this was a surprise to most of my comrades there; yet my intentions in bringing the matter up were political rather than historical in any abstract sense. It was the summer of Anita Bryant's Dade County, Fla. campaign, and I wanted my small pin to be a personal kind of identification, an insistence on my island identity in what appeared a sea of straights. To judge from all the appearances, there wasn't a gay man or lesbian there among the forty or so of us — and it would be awhile before I met Alex or Robbie. It was an odd and disconcerting situation. But I didn't have time to think about it, because right away and in quite a dramatic fashion, my little pink triangle created a situation no one expected.

In general the responses to my pin were favorable enough. Yes, the gay rights struggles going on were important. And yes, many especially wanted me to know their feelings of commitment and solidarity. But there were some who seemed noncommittal and even hostile. Some of the younger men became quite hostile after hearing my explanations. Stand-offish, cool. In conversation they limited their responses to a disinterested 'oh?' or noncommittal half-smile and shrug before moving away. Did my discussion of gay rights bore them? One man said he thought gay rights struggles weren't important. In fact, they were just disruptive. He explained that there have to be priorities, and that the gay movement just drains away energies better spent on struggles that matter. Gays are a tertiary concern. He was sorry, but that was just the way it was. I realized that I was being told to keep my mouth shut — and not in a very nice way either. My view irritated him, and he didn't see any reason to pretend otherwise. There was no point in arguing further. 'What are we supposed to do,' I asked him rhetorically, 'go along quietly to the showers and ovens?' But what a mistake! You're never supposed to be sarcastic in an objective discussion. That was his point of view. After that the homophobic faction replaced patronizing smiles with scowls, which were meant to be warning signs.

But I wasn't alone, and the larger meaning of my situation at the conference became increasingly clear to me. Out of forty or so participants at least half were women — though the institute was, to be sure, male-organized and male-dominated. I saw that women had little or no say in matters of agenda, selection of speakers and so on — in matters of procedure and substance. I noticed too that in the discussion periods after the lectures women were infrequently called on to speak and if they did speak were often interrupted by men. It was taken for granted that male speakers would have more to say than their women colleagues.

I linked all this with my own situation. Most of the women there offered me support and solidarity. True, few men were outright hostile to me. Most were simply as indifferent to the problems of gays as they were to those of women. All this seemed rather strange to me since the announced theme of the conference was 'theory in relation to praxis' or politics and everyday life. I thought more and more of an intervention. And if I couldn't speak for women, I could speak for open gays at the conference, since I was the only one discoverable. I decided I would intervene.

My decision to intervene in our conference was made as a result of a comic misunderstanding that came close to buffoonery. We had met in a room with a long square table that was used for the morning lecture, afternoon discussions, and just about everything else but workshops. I was sitting beside Christine, and Fred was lecturing. He had gotten to one of those characteristically exhilarating and difficult places in his lectures where the language of high French structuralism was coming on fast and furious, and everything was beginning to seem topsy-turvy. Scarcely would a concept present itself in all apparent good faith when it would straightaway become obvious as just a figure;

and the real idea was under, behind or beyond it. Here we strained to comprehend. The old idea hid the new one, it covered it — a worthless abstraction now to be discarded. At this point we stretched our minds to the limit, only to meet with a *real* shock! For we would start to realize that even this new idea was inevitably only the most elegant of all directives to continue the process — toward a content whose wonderful complexity and sophistication would glimmer for an instant only to the most intelligent and sincere among us. How could our exhausted minds keep up the pace? Everyone was in near hysterics trying to follow Fred's flights; and anxiety was beginning to take its toll in a proliferation of blinking eyes, sweating foreheads and near tears of frustration. I did the sensible thing and decided to call it a day. What was the use? Trying so hard to keep up, I was just getting further and further behind. But what's this? Had Christine reached the same decision? As I looked over at her notebook I saw that Christine was absentmindedly doodling. She was drawing circles in the same spot. Sensing a co-conspirator, I passed Christine a note saying I had a terrible headache from too little sleep the night before, and how about her? It was like high school. Would Fred give me a bad grade for not paying attention? But I didn't want to indulge my fantasy, so I contented myself with asking Christine how she was feeling. Christine passed me back a note of her own. Her note said she was tired from staying up too late with a friend and irritated too because all the friend had done was to complain and fight with her. I looked at Christine and gave her what I hoped was my most consoling glance of sympathy. Growing tired of passing notes, we began to slip away into separate worlds of reverie. Fred's voice boomed on in the background, becoming more and more a distant drone. It gradually rose to a conceptual climax I was entirely unaware of. And then it fell. I realized that an entirely new turn or aspect of some theoretical system may well have passed me by. What further treasures might soon be lost beyond recall? Perhaps some startling reversal of expectations would occur, confounding our deepest assumptions about truth values; perhaps Fred even now, the captain of our destinies and true Teddy Roosevelt of our souls, would be leading us o'er hill and dale of some brilliant new terrain whose simple existence I had, in my ignorance, not yet suspected. But why should an uninstructed person such as myself even try? — I asked myself, sinking deeper by the instant into the murky depths of bad faith and somnolence. Great waves of oceanic feeling surged over me and the image of Fred's large frame pulsed back and forth before my failing vision like a consoling mutant monster in a third-rate Japanese science fiction movie. I was an improbably beautiful Japanese princess from the long-lost royal house. Surely Kenji, my brother, would soon come to save me from this predicament! Meanwhile from high atop my mountain sanctuary I can see the searchlights, the terrible search-lights scanning the horizon, lurid flashes from the breakup of great cities, aerial warfare, and the only world I know is dying . . . my heart is filled with deep sorrow! I am inconsolable!

I wake from this daydream abruptly. Christine is pushing a note in my direction, making a funny face. A sort of giggling pout, evidently for my benefit. What's so funny? And I'm trying to rouse myself from the half-sleep I have fallen into. The note reads, 'How would you like to marry Fred? (signed) Christine.' The absurdity of the situation hits us both at the same time. We both recognize we have regressed into a childlike world of no responsibility — of some kind of indolent, complete passivity — and we can't repress our laughter. It is at this moment while we are both laughing — as I now recall — that I make up my mind to intervene in the institute.

For both Christine and myself, I think, the object of these speculations and humor could just as easily have been one of the other lecturers — Stanley or Terry. The point was, we found ourselves 'programmed,' reacting with prearranged thoughts and emotions in just the situation where imposed thoughts or feelings were the most damaging, in a situation where we halfway believed we were thinking our own thoughts. The idea 'What would it be like to marry X?' is, after all, not a spontaneous one. It's prearranged and automatic in a situation where X is a powerful and sometimes older male able to have a real effect on your life — make it better for you, or worse, in some definitive way. For me of course the humor had an added and ironic edge. How could I marry another man? Irrespective of desire and its realization, I could never derive social benefits or privileges from marriage. For Christine, on the other hand, self-advancement through marriage was a real — if unlikely — possibility. This brought me to the bottom line in power relations; it made me realize that if anyone was going to do anything about my situation as the only gay man in the conference it would have to be me. Otherwise my situation wouldn't change. I would have to act!

Public assertiveness was new to me. But I accepted it as a necessary, if not terribly pleasant part of life for everybody. I thought to myself, Assertiveness starts the day you are born — so why be genteel about it? It's what you do in any case, so why not do it successfully? And I made my preparations. First, a strategic alteration of the literary paper I was to read. Then finding out who was in charge of the calendar and arranging a change in the date, so I could read earlier than scheduled. And finally hyping myself up for the actual reading. When the day came I skipped breakfast. I couldn't have eaten anyway for the nervousness. I started taking 5 milligram valiums and enough coffee to wash them down — with glazed doughnuts to create an artistic sugar-hysteria. I figured I wanted to be keyed up enough to make an intervention that would be taken seriously.

I was completely terrified when I started, predictably, but I thought it was better to start conventionally. The text of my paper had been cut here and there and this gave me an opportunity to extemporize, adding explanatory marks as I began to feel more confident. The paper aimed, modestly enough, at articulating gay language usages in a poet whose reputation till now had not included any official recognition of this important aspect of his writing. But as I read what I had prepared, it seemed less and less useful for a polemical occasion. I gradually abandoned my text and tried to make connections between the language of this poet and the language of women. I started to discuss the language of gays and women as symptoms of a still unrecognized oppression. That is where many of the men began to feel uneasy, I noticed. I decided this meant it was time to cut short my reading and get into a discussion. Arms folded and trying to look determined, I looked around the room. I said I thought it was time to bring up the 'problem' of my presence at the conference. The silence that greeted this declaration was deafening.

The storm broke. When I started speaking it was with a lot of accumulated anger. And not so much because of the recent sexist behavior of several of the straight men there either, though that was certainly a starting place. I wanted to speak to an indifference of socialists to problems of gays for a long time. I wanted to speak as a socialist to other socialists about the necessity of making the liberation of gays a goal integral to socialist liberation and revolution. I talked about the treatment of gays in many present-day socialist states. This was a scandal for me. When would socialists protest the work camps for gays in Cuba for instance? I asked why the gay socialist folk singer Holly Near was not allowed into Cuba — the only one refused in a large group of cultural workers — on the grounds of lesbianism. Of all the people, Holly Near, whose socialist credentials were . . . so impeccable! I was very angry, and I asked about many other situations as well — past and present. Then I stopped for a moment. I wanted to cool down and give the audience a chance to do the same. When I began again, I asked for some responses to all this. What was each person's political position with respect to gays and the socialist movement in general? Most people's comments were predictable. Yes, they told us, they were certainly for gays, they felt committed to the gay movement as an important one allied to or within a larger socialist movement. They were sure they could support the gay movement in some way in their own cities and universities. Some were more reserved. They said they weren't sure. They had gay friends whom they liked personally, but honestly they couldn't say what they thought of the gay movement, and they admitted to having reservations. A few in the audience were hostile. One man repeated his opinion that the gay movement was divisive for socialism. Two others walked out.

But generally I was satisfied. I had done what I intended. And if the effect of my intervention was limited, it was also real — it was measured in the expressions of solidarity that came from new friends and allies in the days that followed. I decided that what had happened was something like this. I had learned a little bit about practical action — how to get something done politically — and the others had learned about gay oppression. There seemed to be a reciprocity in this, and we would live and work together for another two weeks. Or perhaps I could put it another way. We were learning to speak each other's languages, in the most literal, ordinary of senses. I would like Gramsci's thought on praxis to be the interpreter of many incidents like this one, and a testimonial to the time, to the daily efforts it always seems to take, to learn another group's language. The rewards should be balanced with that.

In its way my life at the novitiate exemplified this. Successfully or unsuccessfully that religious community dealt with things practically until a set of adequate traditions evolved for most areas in life. And I think our political communities can have this in common with the older communities they have long since overtaken. For both of them flexible networks of codes develop to start solving people's problems in terms of everyday need or common sense. So there begin to be communities, little by little built out of details, small, trifling matters. Is it surprising that jokes and anecdotes will have surprising roles to play here? — and that they may take on pre-figurative meaning for the future of such communities. 'The party is a kind of court,' says Rudolf Bahro, 'and on the site of their differences, it clamps together the competing interests of various groups and levels and makes them mesh toward a higher synthesis.' A preferred ideological technique for living with difficulties or 'muddling through,' you might say — as I think of storytelling. I could cite you a number of examples. What does it mean for instance, recalling my Brother Leo story — to say that a person isn't dead, but has been winged by flights of angels to a happier place above? Small comfort certainly! And I would say the same of less critical problems. We know that narrated disappointments become bearable. They create only the tractable problems of unity.

And to speak of the problems of unity of those days — I remember quite well how Sean and I first admitted our doubts to each other about the value of compulsory confessions with Father Lindsay, the chaplain at Mount LaSalle. Each of us had the impression that our confessions to the chaplain weren't exactly personal, and we felt we could have gotten about the same spiritual benefits by confessing to a pitch man in front of a topless place on Broadway or to the easy-going high school friend everyone once had — the dresser in fine clothing, lady-killer, cheater in geometry classes and con man, borrower of petty cash from friends, entertaining class idler and desperado of safety, who with a shrug of his gentlemanly shoulders kicks through the doors of pretense and at last meets his fate — he becomes a used car salesman. But you know, he could as easily have become the religious version — our Father Lindsay. Well, there's destiny for you, and prudential thought too! The bottom line's minimal effort for a maximum return — the Reverend Father Lindsay, our priest at Mount LaSalle — who like the great white sail of a desultory pleasure craft, lifted and billowed with each passing wind, tacking, accommodating and trimming his course in the sun-filled afternoon of his long life. Our spiritual father, as the Brother Provincial once called him. Sean confided to me that when he went to the priest for confession, Father Lindsay used to huff and puff through the whole thing without a single actual word — as if it was an athletic contest, a test of the confessor's physical condition and prowess demanding signs of great expenditure of energy to insure its sacramental success. And in the same spirit Father Lindsay would eat his dinner at night, groaning and farting wonderful, authoritative farts, sputtering and belching and slavering, giving demonstrative proof to all those within earshot of the immensity of the task that lay before him. At the end of the confession, said Sean, when it came time for the absolution, the chaplain would always heave out a great sigh, indicating the gravity of the sins he had just heard confessed as well as his pessimist's judgment, as an experienced spiritual father and confessor, on Sean's all too clearly will-o'-wisp promises to 'sin no more.' And since confession took place late Saturday afternoon, there would by now be a formidably long line of sinners to confess before the father confessor would be free for his Saturday evening dinner. As minute passed on to inexorable minute, and hour to inexorable hour, the time of the pot roast approached! Father Lindsay, now surprisingly alert and energetic, would pare down his spiritual counsel to the minimum. 'Cheer up, big boy' — says our Father Lindsay — 'Every cloud has a silver lining, now 10 Hail Mary's and a good act of contrition!' And with that he shoos out the newly shriven penitent to make place for the next. The identical scenario repeats itself for Sean the next week. When Sean told me this anecdote at a certain point in our novitiate, I had to laugh, and I had to tell him why. 'But that's what he tells me! It's the advice I always get' — 'Cheer up, big boy, every cloud has a silver lining!'

And it wasn't just that Sean's story seemed funny in itself, though it was of course, assuming as it did that if you confessed larceny or murder, or just a bad case of rudeness during the recreation period, it would be all the same as far as Father Lindsay was concerned for all the attentiveness he displayed as a confessor. What made the story more genuinely funny, I thought, was that it made us the real butt of its humor — it made of all Father Lindsay's penitents the responsible accomplices of their own gulling. Their? Of course I mean 'our!' By its telling and being told the story constituted its hearers as a collectivity of the cheated — at a minimum. Nevertheless if the anecdote revealed a loss to us, it also had another effect, a social effect of some importance. The story armed those cheated with the knowledge of their numbers and gave them an advantage of solidarity against the enemy. Implicit in my laughter at the story — and in the laughter of others — was the making of community through common cause.

After telling me this story Sean wanted to find out if anything similar had happened to Nick. The next Saturday at recreation, after we had all made our confessions, Sean asked Nick what the priest had told him by way of advice. Nick did one of his best parodies, swelling up his cheeks and puffing and panting, with great anticipatory pleasure rubbing an imaginary gut in front of him. 'Cheer up, big boy, every cloud has a silver lining.' We all laughed at the same time, aware of being conspirators.

A collectivity and common praxis — if you will allow me this usage — but not yet the occasion of an earned congratulation. At robing ceremony and at Brother Leo's funeral we gathered and sang —

Ecce quam bonum et quam jucundum
habitare fratres in unum

— 'Behold how good it is and how pleasant when brothers dwell together in unity.' And I was stony and unmoved as Niobe weeping for her children, refusing to be comforted. Doesn't something get lost in reconciliations like this? I am fearful for them. Oh, I believe in the new collectivity and its praxis. When I read my Rudolf Bahro and my Gramsci I am practically leaping and shouting for joy — 'O the new Jerusalem!' And yet — I can never quite say 'Thank you, Jesus.' I remain ungrateful, suspicious, mistrustful. But in the end I continue to hope, not for the banishment of these words of community from the human heart, but that they learn to live a glorious and beautiful life for the first time.

Jokes, songs, stories, anecdotes. The common repertory, the common practice.

I think it was Stanley at the conference who repeated the ancient joke about the elderly New York ladies meeting on the street and exchanging news items, divided neatly into 'good' and 'bad' categories. 'First the bad news, I found out my son's a homosexual.' 'And what's the good news?' 'He married a doctor!' A chestnut, yes. But when a straight Jewish man tells it to an ex-Catholic gay man, doesn't it mean some measure of warmth and trust? — and on both sides. One hopes that, as one hopes they are both socialists. Underneath is a history of disaster for three groups. And that is why the joke remains diffident, defensive, self-deprecatory. Naturally a person would be naïve to think of this sort of thing as more than a verbal solution. But isn't it a kind of mustering of forces? A precondition maybe; a prehistory.

My intervention might have come to nothing at all, if it hadn't been reciprocal in some way; if it hadn't begun to consort with all of the trivial, the historical, the ritualistic of the group, even its gossip. There was an unspoken quid pro quo of language to be learned — beginning with a repetition of certain words. Songs for instance, like the Internationale, which, as it happened, I hadn't learned yet. Even liberties of a more personal kind, which could be hoped to testify to kindliness. And so, for example, I worked out a version of Stanley's idiosyncracies as a lecturer, meaning it to function as both compliment and entertainment — a mimetic distortion of an original working class vowel system combining Jewish-style sarcasm and torrential verbal allusiveness with academic syntax fractured into provocations of laughter by arm or body movements of show-offy, serious solidarity. What a credit to all concerned! — or so one hoped. Somewhere underneath this was the unspoken recognition of details, their ability to make or unmake a commitment.

With the acknowledgment of details came the acknowledgment of the body. It seemed to follow, because details are concrete. With the body — and there is no alternative in the last instance — you join the others in love and in friendship, or in struggle. And the realization of this home truth is what finally made me critical of my earlier intervention at our conference, just as it had long before that — with the obsessionally missed sexual opportunities that, as I discovered, had characterized my relations with men in my novitiate years, my hippie period and all through my twenties.

This led to a second intervention, my last, which happened soon afterwards. All day long there were words at our institute, words and more words. Abstractions, theories. After dinner we couldn't help but want to be without words and relax. So we played volleyball. But the point was, it wasn't just a game. It was volleyball because — it *had* to be. Isn't it strange to you — it is to me! — how irrational some people can get about their chosen sport? Think about growing up and the high school math teacher — male — who tells his students — *believing* it — that 'football prepares you for life.' Or how many intellectuals — also male! — do you know who tell you you 'have to go to the baseball games because it's part of American culture — an example of the things you'll learn so you'll appreciate your own culture more.' But then you find out you have to like volleyball too — because it's part of a *socialist* tradition. Volleyball, it turns out, is a politically correct choice because, as you are told, it hasn't been 'commercialized' and it's 'never a *spectator* sport.' Consequently, everyone is obliged to participate. Furthermore, men and women can play it equally well and there are no 'stars' — so it's a recreation you ought to have *fun* at! At any rate that's the ideology. In practice of course things may not work out that way. They didn't at our institute. In fact volleyball brought out hidden conflicts that had never been resolved, and often were not even discussed. Volleyball turned out to extend certain power realities based on sex.

It wasn't intended to be that way, but that's the way it turned out. There was even a spirit of generosity among many of our participants. Stanley, for instance — who discounted his disconcerting and aggressive appearance with jokes at his own expense and a fumbling body language that reassured the timid among us that he wasn't out to harm. Or Sonia, the responsible one, who organized things — who took responsibility for all the cajoling and corralling that had to be done if you wanted to get enough people to make up a game. She called this 'being a mother hen,' deprecatingly, afraid this might make her seem less attractive to the men there who didn't like women they thought were 'pushy.' And Patsy — whose generosity consisted remarkably and noticeably in a daily effort to get through the game to be a good sport, since it was a group activity. Against her own obvious inclinations she made more consistent efforts to be a good team player than anyone I can remember, in her way heroic. But for most of the men, the volleyball game was a way of relaxing, as often as not at someone else's expense.

For me relaxing meant going for a nice long walk. Something on the quiet side. But certainly not something with loud noises and people knocking up against you. What was wrong with going to a movie to relax, or just lolling about on the grass for recreation? And the violence bothered me. Why did there have to be this cutthroat competition, I wondered? It bothered me when some of the men used their elbows against others to hurt them. It bothered me particularly when they would elbow women. Or push around men who were shorter or less well-built or timid. And it bothered me a lot when this happened to me. One man particularly, I remember, used to slam the volleyball over the net singling out Patsy, an 'obvious' target who would drop the ball and not be able to return it. This she didn't do all the time but did more and more as time went on — from anxiety. When I complained to him that I thought this was unfair, he said he just wanted to tease Patsy. Didn't I think people should be able to take a little teasing? I hated him for saying this. In my view this man was systematically violent — and just as well as Patsy I might have been the object of his attack.

And this is what actually happened. There was another man there who had decided to be the group expert in volleyball rules, because, as he pointed out, he always scored more than anyone, no matter what team he was chosen for. He did this by deciding that anyone playing next to him obviously wouldn't have the nerve to return fast serves successfully. When he saw a serve or fast ball coming anywhere in his general direction he would just move in, pushing everybody else out of the way — to make certain, as he explained, that the point wouldn't be lost. But with this roughing up of people on a regular basis, other players too began to become upset. This behavior went on for some time.

His victims usually got red in the face and yelled, telling him angrily to stop it. This would make a definite impression, but not a lasting one. Embarrassed and profusely apologizing, he'd be very contrite and stop his behavior for all of 10 or 15 minutes. Then he was back to doing what he had done before. Here was a person I genuinely hated. A real bully. Childhood experiences of being mistreated in similar ways came back to me with a new force. I was truly shocked — how could this happen *here* at a conference of committed socialists? Yet here was this terrible thing actually happening, even if in theory it *shouldn't* have been happening. But what to do?

The day I decided to do something just happened to be the day David and I were returning from our famous walk. Earlier I broke off — though not rudely, I hope — to tell you I'd return to complete my account of this game after explaining some of the tensions involved. The ball that went sailing by our noses that day, so uncivilly ending our tranquil walk, seemed to me to sum up in itself all the aggressions of the game itself as well as those of our obnoxious teammate. I accepted the invitation to join the game with a firm purpose to act that very day. Exactly how, I wasn't sure; I just knew, I would do something! Then I remembered, Sonia and I and some others had a contingency plan — which was begging to be put into effect. Why not now?

That day our plan went into action. First the ball gets served and comes over the net pretty much in my direction. As usual, pushy teammate moves over into my space to return it, yelling to everybody in sight 'I'll get it, I'll get it' — meaning of course to get out of the way. Only what happened was I didn't. I stayed there, my shoulders hunched up on the assumption that I would be the 'accidental' recipient of one of his elbows. I grabbed at the ball and somehow caught it.

That was it, the whole strategy we had. I didn't return the ball or do anything with it at all, I just stood there holding it close to my chest so nobody could take it away. Let them think whatever they wanted. I was going to keep the ball so the game couldn't go on, I announced, and then prudently moved to the sidelines out of reach of my pushy teammate to give a little speech, saying I was awfully tired of certain people's selfish, pushy volleyball manners. I said they were doing the same things in our game that they had done before. They obviously must think it was alright to push people or take advantage of people or tease them or embarrass them. Apparently this was just good clean fun to them since it was only a game. I said I thought this was dumb and unfair, and I wanted to talk about it.

That was my second intervention. And I think the only reason my pushy teammate didn't beat me up at this point was because of my strategy of talking it over with Sonia and the other women beforehand. They said they'd back me. So the prearranged plan was when I finished my protest Sonia would come over and take the ball herself and basically agree with me, saying we ought to quit for the day and talk about this, since there were other people who had similar complaints. So when Sonia came over and made a speech proposing a group discussion of the dispute, nobody seemed surprised, even the jerk with the pushy elbows and grabby hands. Later Sonia told me he had apologized. I asked her when, since I hadn't heard it. She said that was because his voice was low and to give him credit for trying. I said I did, but if you were a socialist wasn't the point to make people and things *change*? She said it was. Only he wasn't the enemy, was he? I admitted probably he wasn't, probably the enemy was Standard Oil, Exxon, imperialism, etc. etc. — only I admitted this with some reluctance.

Well. But it is the basic question after all. Who is the enemy and who isn't? It's a question that recalls an incident that didn't develop until the second institute, but which, when it did, complicated the question with desire so that I realized there couldn't ever be a personal answer to this question — but only a collective one.

Who was the enemy? Not Fred, for sure, though we had feuded semi-publicly over feminism and the gay movement. And certainly not Robbie in any sense, even when I discovered someplace in the middle of things that his idea of our relationship didn't match mine. Probably not even 'X' — as I'll call him — whose sexism and possessiveness went unabated and untroubled by all our criticism. Strangely it was X who unknowingly brought me to think of the collective aspect of the relations of friendship — and relations of hate — that desire continuously abets and subverts without for the most part being given the credit. I thought of the arrangements of love in a new light — less personally in some ways.

X was the cause of this. He was jealous of his friend Y, his friend of some years and together they managed to bring on a whole new French bedroom farce starring Peter in the lead with Robbie, David and me in supporting roles. The end result was thought provoking for me; my sense of community began to take on the limitations of real bodies, real people. If — to look ahead for a moment — Peter hadn't left the apartment, I wouldn't have thought I was alone. And if I hadn't thought I was alone in the apartment . . . well, there's the key as far as I'm concerned. The preliminaries in all this were these. Alex had joined Robbie for dancing at the cowboy bar we usually went to. And as for David — whom we left without too many formalities on the occasion of Party Night — no one knew where he was. So he'll now be seen to play a new role here — the one who doesn't understand anything himself, so that other people will start to. In that capacity he takes on my function as storyteller. The meaning of the story is always getting away from you, becoming what you didn't intend.

Now let's set the stage. You can think of it as Act IV of the Marriage of Figaro — in which everyone is unmasked as someone else. Peter is out of the apartment because of the simple fact that the phone has rung three times, not two and not four. By prearrangement two rings is supposed to mean 'Don't come, I can't get away.' Four is 'Oh don't bother, I can go to your place.' And three — wonderful three! — is 'Meet me at the elevator right now!' Such were the precautions due to X's jealousy. So when the phone rings three times, Peter is halfway out the door, already on his way. Evidently, you have to be prepared to act fast and be inventive when you are seeing someone whose boyfriend is insanely jealous. And more often than not — as it happened — these lovers' trysts took place with the elevator jammed between floors. Anxious embraces alternate with harried glances over the shoulder. The signal lights on the control panel are going crazy, indignantly demanding the return of this bower of bliss to other floors for more respectable uses. An embarrassing, compromising position, to be sure — but what a tribute to the eternal resourcefulness of Love, wouldn't you say? Love, love, love — it always finds a way. Unfortunately — these stolen kisses are not to last long. Y's jealous boyfriend X gets wind of this scheme and he's furious. He becomes archetypal. He storms in to Y — 'Is it true? Tell me!!' 'Oh, no no no!' 'It *is* true, I know it's true, admit it!' 'Oh all right then, it is.' And she promises never to do such a thing again. Armed with this admission from the beloved, X now seeks out friend Peter. Explains he's not a jealous or possessive person, but he does want an admission of the truth of the matter. Confronts P with Y's confession. Dio — thinks our friend Pete — the game's up! What will he do? Confesses. And what exemplary contrition, remorse he displays. Promises never, never never to do it again, etc. Exit the now complacent and placated X. So is there a moral here? How I wish it was edifying! After only an hour or two the phone rings again — three times. Oh l'amour, l'amour! Toujours l'amour.

In this development Peter had left the apartment as per above. What were Robbie's plans for the evening? They were more mysterious. He and Alex had joined some friends and left for the cowboy bar. I was beginning to develop classical symptoms, wondering if our romance was already on the rocks. I was becoming quite despondent thinking about it when I decided to do something quite practical, sensible, to cheer myself up. I started to read the latest Kristeva. Dreadful thing! Do I have to read this to be considered an educated person? But wait a minute. Maybe I can just ask David to tell me about it. 'David' — I call out across to the other side of our duplex apartment, the side he's sharing with Peter. There's no answer. Silence. David must have changed his mind. He's with Robbie and Alex. 'Well I hope *they're* having a good time because *I'm* not!' — and start running a shower. 'Why should I stay home studying when everybody else is out having a good time? I'm going dancing!'

The knock at the door comes right after I turn on the shower. It's on Peter and David's side, so it's obviously not for me. Still — who could it be? I'm curious. I put a towel around me and decide to open the door. 'Janet Leigh, the shower scene' — I suddenly think a little histrionically.

But out in the corridor it's only Fred. He's gotten back from the city 50 miles away. He can't find anybody, he says. Where is everybody? Where is Peter? No one's in, so we chat a little in amiable fashion, though officially we're still fighting. We're uneasy, I see, but polite. Each in our own way we're trying to be agreeable — what else is there to do? I remember Peter's recommendation earlier, couldn't I make an effort to be nicer? Somehow the word gets all mixed up and applied a new way. Fred is starting to look so *nice!* He's wearing a nice country Western cowboy shirt with small pearl buttons, and that looks nice too. As I look at Fred he starts to look nicer and nicer until he glows. He's glowing with niceness. He's looking quite attractive. I feel I'm in the middle of a poem about the future or the sun, or something glowing and tender or maybe all of these things mixed together. I feel I am growing more reddish myself with every moment. What strange feelings! Would it be possible then, I think, to make only a *partial* reconciliation, a step in the right direction, perhaps a gesture that says, 'good will and at least not enemies.' I volunteer these feelings out loud — a person can only try. 'You've done a lot for me, you know.' He steps back — puzzled? skeptical? 'What did I ever do?' 'You taught me — your books did, even before I met you.' I feel slightly idiotic, maybe this was a stupid idea, and feel myself growing more anxious. With the anxiety there's red all over my body. The intimacy is growing unbearable, and I'm conscious I'm standing there with only a towel on. It's a flirtatious moment and an impossible situation. I should end it. 'My shower is running...' — a little vaguely, smiling, hoping to be friendly. Everything's OK, isn't it? And I point back into the apartment. In a few more moments we've said good-night. Fred's on his way to his place to go to sleep, I'm going to the bar in town. Good-night. 'See you in the morning.' 'See you.' And shut the door. Strange, does nice mean the color red? How — I wonder. Oh! — remembering Peter's advice. Nice a 'politically correct' term? Become one? Not very exact, I guess. Well. A shirt with pearl buttons. Nice for dancing, and that's nice too, isn't it? Now myself I look better in a sweater maybe, preppy, but not too New Wave — as I go back to the shower. I finish it up. Get dressed.

I pass David's room. He's still there! 'Hi,' he greets me with a smile. 'I thought you were out! Were you here the whole time? Didn't you hear me talking to Fred!' He puts down a dog-eared *Des Chinoises* by Julia Kristeva. 'I didn't hear a thing.' I'm astounded but decide not to show it. David's a real intellectual, gets wrapped up in his books and doesn't notice a thing. I'm glad to have company now and decide to defer my project of going out. I tell David all about my conversation with Fred. Time goes by, and David smokes one cigarette after another. I decide to drink some of Peter's wine in a dirty plastic glass I've found — one glass after another. David meanwhile has stopped studying in order to be sociable, helps himself to one of the stockpile of cupcakes on hand, and we trade complaints about our respective love lives. Things don't seem so awful, I've stopped thinking about Robbie. Oh everything's starting to be so nice, why don't we go on out to the cowboy bar and join the others? Why not, it's a terrific idea. Let's do it!

So we do. And the bar that night is perfect, it's heaven. The old persons are in the old persons' bar, the students are in the student bar and even the white-shoe men have joined laughing bee-hive ladies in their bar. We go to the cowboy bar. When we walk in they're playing my favorite song. 'You picked a fine time to leave me, Lucille!' and everything's begun well. 'Roll over Beethoven.' Look, there's Fred talking theory to Jim K, who appears happy at the opportunity to soak up more knowledge, and to Christine, who just looks bored right now! Why did Fred change his mind and come out? Everything's so nice! 'Ghost Riders in the Sky' — a somber moment now, for remembering the serious side of life. X is talking with Y — their moral earnestness now evident — will they become reconciled again? I wonder. The glittering Christmas tree lights, December holdovers into a hot, flat, uncomfortable midwest summer, spell out alternate messages in red and yellow — 'yes' 'no' 'yes' 'no'. Christmas in July.

Meanwhile the small cowboy band plays its final set. David gets up to make a phone call, and someone puts on the juke box. First it's oldies. Remember 'Wake up Little Susie?' Then another Everly Brothers — 'Sugar in the Morning.' In the evening! At the suppertime! — I fill it out. Remember when you wanted to be Phil Everly's own sweet sugar, but you couldn't tell anyone? They wouldn't understand. 'Be my little honey and love me all the time.' Well *I* was certainly willing! Things are warming up now. Ray Charles, the wonderful Ray Charles from college days, I was a sophomore. He tells us to see the girl with the red dress on. She can shake that thing, all night long! Yay, I'm feeling really good now! Peter is up on the dance floor, he's dancing with June — they're leading the way. What's that? Oh, Dolly Parton, I mouth it with delight at the same time as Alex — 'Two Doors Down!' And we're all in a party mood. Dolly's telling it like it is.

Where's Judy and Tom? There they are in the corner — as Gloria Gaynor comes on — it's 'I Will Survive,' wonderful song of heroism and camp melodrama. They wave good-naturedly over at our table, 'You young folks go on out and have a good time!' How can they be so *domestic* when they're not as old as I am? — but they're wrapped up in each other. Then — none of us can stay in our seats any longer. It's

'We Are Family' with Sister Sledge, the disco hit of the whole summer. Suddenly everyone in the institute is on their feet dancing. Everything coalesces; it's the moment we've been waiting for. The alcohol, the music, the time — everything so right! So exactly right, and we're all together. Reserved Tony is smiling and dancing with June. Wonderful. Alongside them Alex, Robbie and I make a threesome — which is certainly wonderful too! Boldly Tony steps under and though us and joins the surprised Alex, and from the corner of my eye I can see that June and Mimi are together. And I'm partners with Robbie. He makes me forget all my earlier worries, he's treating me right and I feel so good. Then slowly we wheel — and all take new partners. We must have time for everything in the world, I think, the disco beat is so fantastic! It goes on and on and won't stop. Is this what happiness might mean? In a circle now, we've all thought the same thing — we join hands and we're together. We're dancing and dancing, and there'll never be an end.

But then I see David over at our table, looking paler than usual, I think. He's back from his phone call. What's the matter? I go over to find out. Briefly he tells me. There's a friend, he says. He's been trying to reach her all evening. He knows it's sudden, but he's taking the Greyhound out early in the morning, before we're up. Wants to meet her in the lake area near the Canadian border. Sorry he didn't have more time, but wanted to say goodbye now.

I shake off the liquor in a second. I'm sincerely shocked. It's so sudden, I guess. I don't feel like any more dancing, and it's almost closing time.

Walking back to the apartment now we make our affectionate good-byes to David — Alex and Robbie and I. We'll all see each other

in a year, we promise. We do mean it. Then he's off. Strange evening! —
to be put into motion by, let's see now, jealousy, lust, friendship . . . and,
well, politics. How do they mix? Somber, serious. Reaching the apartment, good-night! good-night! — and then by yourself to be alone,
lights off. We'll talk in the morning.

As for myself in the present, I recall with anxiety each book left un-
read, poem not finished, friendships left fallow, political actions not
taken. How to understand this. Dream: I walk into an upland mead-
ow, opening up to fields of flowers. Hurry up, Bruce! — from a distance. Taking a step, I wade in. They're waist high. Don't slow down
now! They're glorious — but go on!

Afterword
Bruce Boone

The name "Century of Clouds" is from an Apollinaire poem. It's an image for the transient, for what passes. The image still seems rich to me, especially now. Time calls attention to itself, and the imagery of clouds encourages readers to date this book through the passage of time. Whatever politics are in these pages may or may not be meaningful now. And that's fine. The politics, as all politics, will pass like the tiny white splinters left over from a dandelion when a child blows on it, scattering its fluff to the winds.

Still, if the politics are dated can they also still play a role? In my book, a politics once polemical wants to be emotional, perhaps a vehicle to joy, elation, even ecstasy. In my own experience politics emerged first as a purpose: I, we (Marxists), wanted something to happen, we wanted to change something. But in writing, emotion takes charge of the politics, so everything gets turned around: the political becomes the means to the production of affect in the reader, just as affect and emotion likewise lead to politics.

The book centers on emotions. At the same time it's a record of analyzed ecstasies. The vehicle is words, and nothing but words, words I tried to employ in such a way so as to lead readers to the possibility of their own ecstasy. There is ecstasy, but there are also the devices that trigger it, and neither ecstasy nor those devices can function without each other in creating stories that open up, so to speak, the skycover above us — to some stellar beyond. The means of doing this is the work's inventiveness. And its value is at least in part determined by rationality and technique. Emotion in itself remains ineffable. To make it speak, some scaffolding is needed, commentary and analysis for instance (as in *Century of Clouds*): that is, a calculation of means or some other unobtrusive mechanism that will seduce readers into feeling whatever I, the writer, intended them to feel — as if emotions arising within the readers were in fact their very own, just now discovered by them, and not those of me, the writer.

Think of the loveliest pages of Rousseau. A person comes away from reading his *Confessions* with a strong sense that these were in fact Rousseau's own feelings, emotions he really experienced himself, and not factitious in any way! This direct experience of emotion is often thought to be romantic. Is a book of joy then to be defined as a romantic book? But what if every ecstasy is inexorably and immediately analyzed? For me, the so-called alienation of analysis does the opposite of what Brecht wanted and instead makes the book emotionally as "infectious" as Brecht wanted his own work not to be. What do you remember about *The Good Woman of Szechuan* if not her progress from good intentions to greed? Did you really learn Marxist lessons about the ideological wobbliness of the petite bourgeoisie? In my book, the alienation that becomes analysis is hardly about words or concepts at all, or if it is, it's only insofar as they convey emotion. In the end, it's emotion that counts. Just emotion.

What else but the winds of strong emotion are capable of propelling you into eternity? To construct an invisible mechanism that succeeds in prodding readers into the fabrication of their own ecstatic destiny is, paradoxically, to make them genuinely feel. So I think of these ecstasies as being guided by "writerly shamanism." What do I mean by that?

. Let me use a famous example from history: the case of the ineffable or unspeakable emotions in Apuleius's *Transformations* (aka *The Golden Ass*). Apuleius was the first in antiquity to introduce "the autobiographical" as a genre, a genre that stood on its own two feet. With his book, emotions were introduced into prose writing that beforehand weren't possible — emotions you could really identify with. Now, for the first time in prose, a real subject becomes possible, a genuine 'I', serving guess what? . . . well, emotion! The place of the autobiographical is similar in this way to that of the political or the analytical. Look at Apuleius's description of his initiation into the Isis cult. Without an autobiographical frame his description of this event wouldn't have had the hectic exclamatory emotional quality that it does and instead would have been "dead on arrival" in real-emotion terms — like the Hellenistic novels that preceded him, dead! "I reached the threshold of the underworld, I traveled through the elements, the cosmos," Apuleius writes. Now, in this account of his initiation ceremony, it is above all the autobiographical that provides us with a stage on which our hero can "oooh" and "ahh" like any other actor, and by means of which he can rope you into feeling the same emotions he's feeling. You find yourself in a whirligig of ecstasy and terror. "I descended all the way to the threshold of the other world and I flew back through the flotsam and jetsam of the elements making up the cosmos!" For the first time, in the western tradition at least, we're lucky enough to be invited to "cofeel" with the narrator, to feel out his emotions as if they were our own.

In *Century of Clouds*, I wanted to offer you a way of feeling the same emotions of elation and joy I experienced myself — or (to a degree) fabricated. Readers, is writing really the same as truth-telling? (In Hesiod the muses admit they "sometimes lie"). The ability to do this kind of emotional writing requires a calculus of rigorous effects, a special technique — in my case in the book, it was commentary and analysis — as well as honesty.

To be frank, I started out with quite noble aspirations, and always in the name of politics, so that my efforts would never besmirch the noble name of politics. But after writing a bit, I saw that my supposedly true account of some particular emotion sometimes failed to be emotionally moving and worse, was boring. I did what we all do, that is all writers (and probably all humans). Thus *Century of Clouds* isn't without its white lies. Sometimes I do fabricate, I make things up, put things into language sheerly for the sake of beauty and the emotion — and to hell with the truth. Reader, I know you are scandalized — shocked I say, shocked!

So let's put it a different way. In the normal course of things it's the cerebellum that masters emotions. To write in order to give the reader access to heights of transport is to reverse things and to harness the intellect into the service of emotion. To elicit emotions, you need a kind of false subject that will make the reader comfortable. Traditionally it was the work first of shamanism and now it's the task of psychoanalysis to unravel that false "I." The work of writing is the opposite — to reconstitute this phoney "I."

If shamanism is well known for accessing emotions, is it any less famous for possessing certain tools of rationality that, historically, through all cultures and times, have actually, as with the figure of the psychopomp, led its clients to transport, ecstasy through mantras and chants. This closes the gap between emotion and expression, or emotion and communication. Apollo's Delphic priestess called Pythia for instance was perfectly able to feel things of abundant depth whenever Apollo began riding his mount, and did she ever rant and shriek at the god's possession of her! (It took its toll.) Still, tradition had made sure there were always trained scribes available just off-stage listening to these ravings and translating them into what was clearest and most perfectly comprehensible at the time: Greek hexameters. This way, as shamanism discovered, you can have your cake and eat it: ineffable and supreme ecstasy, but an intelligible message as well. There's a kind of vatic transmission (Blake) in western poetry and sometimes in prose that has followed this pattern — a combination of highest ecstasy with rationality giving significance to an emotion that it might not otherwise be capable of. This as a way of making what is incomprehensible comprehensible.

What was effective for ancient shamanism may be equally so for the contemporary world. First there was shamanism, then oracles, now there's writing — all attempting to deliver the same thing: emotions. Doesn't rationality then have an enormous task before itself? There is a whole line of thought concerning such productions that goes from Pythagoras to Plato and from Plato to Plotinus — all concerned first and foremost with an elucidation, that is analysis, of transport or elation. The rationality of *Century of Clouds* is that of a somewhat dated Marxism. Also time-stamped is its concern with boosting the fortunes of the New Narrative movement of the 1980s. Yet from all that datedness there remains something worth keeping in my estimate.

As the word "clouds" already suggest largeness, I'll add one more thing here. There was and remains — wonderful! — a certain largeness to this whole era. It was after all a time of Marxism, feminism, gay rights, black struggles, the beginnings of an environmental awareness all marking this era in question. So too with the political — large, large, large! In this way I'd see in my book a product of its own time. In the '60s and '70s, before globalization, there was still a germ of this in the largeness I am speaking of. We looked at things from the standpoint of a whole world, a whole humanity — and I see in this sensibility something worth looking at. It was that globality that has put its stamp on *Century of Clouds*.

I wanted to write large. Who didn't? And it was largeness, specifically, that I was conscious of when writing *Century*. The writing of this book suffused me with joy. I felt I saw myself among spiral galaxies. I recognized my humanity in the largeness of phenomena. I lived in the Crab Nebula.

The emotion of ecstasy is tied to globality — the capital letters of emotion: this is what I thought in CENTURY: I wrote as in a trance. The work is shamanic in that sense. Pervaded by joy. Though there's a plethora of negative emotions (anger, resentment, etc.) alongside, naturally, but it's above all a sense of joy and transport that structures this book.

Or is this another way of saying the face of youth, the hormones surging inside you then? There remains in me some wish — which may or may not come into being in book form — to match *Century*'s youthful joy with another emotion, but a darker kind. *Century*, which is light, deserves its dark companion, and some day it may find it.

Can we in the meantime just walk together a few hours, you and I — as large now as the skies, brows knitting and pushing away clouds in our reading of this work?

Where then, and when? And from here?

★　★　★　★　★

This book is thankfully dedicated to Madeleine Boone, the author's loving and beloved and encouraging mother.

Thanks too, and heartfelt at that, should be given to many others, of which only a few alas can be singled out here by name, for reasons of space. These would be Bob Gluck, for friendship and for teaching me to write better. Jim Mitchell, for publishing the first edition of this and generously giving permission for us to publish this edition. Stephen Motika and to Nightboat, for enthusiasm, dedication and so much hard work, plus some extras—all of which have succeeded in finally making this book happen as a second edition after being out of print 27 long years. My late teacher, Issan, for his enormously large heart, that began to anchor my life and teach at least bare rudiments of a compassion. Rob Halpern, for his editorial help and his preface. Last but not least, Fredric Jameson, the great thinker of our day, who helped me to perform the transit from only feeling to both thinking and feeling, and the two together, I hope!

Ghosts preoccupy Bruce Boone, who lives alone now in San Francisco with only dog Sadie. He wants to write a love story about Jamie, his late beloved. But they come at him like bats.

The Lives of a Spirit/Glasstown: Where Something Got Broken by Fanny Howe

The Truant Lover by Juliet Patterson (Winner of the 2004 Nightboat Poetry Prize)

Radical Love: Five Novels by Fanny Howe

Glean by Joshua Kryah (Winner of the 2005 Nightboat Poetry Prize)

The Sorrow And The Fast Of It by Nathalie Stephens

Envelope of Night: Selected and Uncollected Poems, 1966-1990 by Michael Burkard

In the Mode of Disappearance by Jonathan Weinert (Winner of the 2006 Nightboat Poetry Prize)

Your Body Figured by Douglas A. Martin

Dura by Myung Mi Kim

The All-Purpose Magical Tent by Lytton Smith (Winner of the 2007 Nightboat Poetry Prize)

Absence Where As (Claude Cahun and the Unopened Book) by Nathanaël (Nathalie Stephens)

Tiresias: The Collected Poems by Leland Hickman

FORTHCOMING TITLES

In the Function of External Circumstances by Edwin Torres

)((eco (lang)(uage(reader)) edited by Brenda Iijima

Poetic Intention by Édouard Glissant

A Tonalist by Laura Moriarty

Ghost Fargo by Paula Cisewski (Winner of the 2008 Nightboat Poetry Prize)

This book was made possible by a grant from the Topanga Fund, which is dedicated to promoting the arts and literature of California.

The following individuals have supported the publication of this book. We thank them for their generosity and commitment to the mission of Nightboat Books:

Kazim Ali
Loretta and Robert Dorsett
Photios Giovanis
Elizabeth Motika
Benjamin Taylor

In addition, this book has been made possible, in part, by a grant from the New York State Council on the Arts Literature Program.

NYSCA
New York State Council on the Arts